I0677247

THE SCENT OF CLOSURE

This is a work of fiction. Names, characters, places, and incidents either are the product of the author's imagination or are used fictitiously. Any resemblance to actual persons, living or dead, events, or locales is entirely coincidental.

Copyright © 2022 Skyler Talley

All rights reserved. No part of this book may be reproduced or used in any manner without written permission of the copyright owner.

Book cover design by Valerie Aethra

First paperback edition February 2022

ISBN 978-0-578-25866-9 (paperback)

ISBN 978-0-578-25867-6 (ebook)

skylertalley.com

To the ones who are still searching for their happily ever after

PART 1: THE RETURN

falling back home

As I sit in the taxi cab pulling away from the airport, the only things on my mind are 1) how summer is ruined and 2) how I'll never recover from this heartbreak. I should be worrying about college, but that's the last thing on my mind. Besides, I have all summer to figure that out.

"What brings you to California?" asks the driver.

My ruined relationship, for starters. But it's more than just that. It's the fact that I've lost everything: my love, myself, my career, my sanity.

A year ago, if you would've told me I'd be falling apart in the back of a taxi cab on my way home from college, I never would have believed you.

I was the one who had it all figured out: Rebecca Dae, the prom queen in high school, the one with all the potential. In college, I had friends, I was happy, and I had my whole future laid out in front of me. I'd always been fun, unshakable, stable. And now look at me.

"Home," I answer, trying to keep my shaky voice in check. "I'm going home."

It's not a long drive from the Orange County airport. Driving down the freeway this time of night is peaceful because darkness settles over the world, making the city lights out-shine the stars. I'm thankful the stars are hidden tonight- I can't bear the painful memories they accompany.

I play games with the cars around us and pretend we're horses in a race, edging toward the finish line. I pretend there are prizes if I win.

But at some point, I get nauseous.

The cars move lanes away from me, and we can't play anymore.

The streetlights flash at me like strobe lights, making me feel dizzy.

I want to go home. Home before there was Andy Bynes. I need someone to stop me from falling, someone to catch me before I hit the ground.

I can't do it myself.

"You look pale, miss," says the driver as he turns on the air for me.

But we arrive at my house before I can feel the chill set in.

He drives off, and I'm left standing unsure in the driveway, leaning on my luggage for support to stand. My feet start moving, and I drag my suitcase behind me up the hill of the driveway.

Standing at the front door reminds me how I used to

stand in Andy's doorway, pleading with him to save me. And he always did. It was like a game we were addicted to.

I'd cry, and he'd wipe the sadness from my cheeks.

We didn't start like this.

But I'm at a doorway again, and who's going to save me now?

The door swings open before I knock twice. Mom can sense one of her kids from a mile away. She didn't know I was coming, but she knew me. She knew I'd be here, looking for someone to pick up my broken pieces.

"Come in," she says. "You're home now."

And I stumble inside.

The house hasn't changed since I left. A row of my family's shoes sits at the side of the door, the wooden floors are spotless as ever, and the peony curtains wave under the breeze of the air conditioning.

The rest of the family sits at the table, eating what looks like lasagna made by Dad. He's been branching out from his usual Korean meals for the last six months. He's sent me pictures every night of what they eat. Sometimes it looks edible; other times, I'm glad I'm across the country so I don't have to be anywhere near that plate. Dad making food is already a risky choice, even with the foods he's used to. But my siblings don't look like they're wincing too much, so maybe he's become a better cook since the last time I visited.

"Rebecca!" shouts a voice.

There's a flurry of movement as June latches onto me,

hugging me tight as she can. She's what I missed most while I was at college in Boston. I missed my sister's skinny arms giving me great big bear hugs, and I missed the way her face lights up when she tells me about the latest gossip at her school.

Even though she's in remission, leukemia gave her dyspnea and reduced lung capacity as a parting gift, which still forces her to wear a cannula strapped across her pretty face.

I kiss her forehead.

"Are you staying all summer?" she asks excitedly.

I put on a grin. "Yeah. You, me, and Griffin all summer." The sibling trio reunited at last.

June squeals. "There's a new jewelry shop by the pier. Can we go there tomorrow?"

She keeps talking even though I don't answer her.

I don't want to go to the beach tomorrow. I won't be able to enjoy walking down the shore without remembering him. I won't be able to go to our ice cream place.

We ruined the magic of summer.

There's always something so special about summer when you're younger.

But now, I don't see the appeal.

I'm disgusted by its false sense of security. I hate the way the humid heat brings celebration along with it.

Earlier at the airport, I watched groups of young travelers seeking fun at the beach. I loathed their optimism, the way they laughed at everything. Tans and bikinis were all they could think of.

But give them a few days. Wait until sunburns scorch their flesh. Wait until some girl gets their hopes up and then crushes it with a smile. Let them wait until bombs destroy their hope, turning their beaches to graves and blood.

Come autumn, we'll all go back to despising our lives, so why let summer get in the way of our despair?

Still, there's a part of me that wishes I could be like the tourists who flock here for the season. I wish I could enjoy summer again without carrying around this pain.

"Maybe Andy could even come," June says, oblivious to my inattention.

His name snaps me out of my thoughts.

"No, he's not coming," I say sharply.

Griffin, my younger brother, leaves the table to join us. He wears a gaming shirt that's three sizes too large for him.

"Where's Andy?" he asks.

"I don't think Rebecca wants to talk about him," Mom offers, trying to change the subject. I haven't told her about the breakup, but she's intuitive like that. Maybe all moms are.

"Why?" Griffin says, oblivious as ever. "Andy was gonna teach me to surf this summer."

Welcome to the graveyard of failed plans.

"Is Andy okay?" June asks nervously.

"Yeah, I want him to take me back to the comic book store," Griffin says.

Dad joins the family circle, late to the conversation. "How is Andy doing?"

"Stop talking about Andy!" I yell. "From here on out, let's not say his name."

I feel my cheeks flush.

All eyes are on me.

"We're not together anymore," I say quietly.

Four pairs of arms wrap around me, and I try not to break down amidst them.

"It's good to have you home," Dad says.

dr. sherman

While I watch movies on my laptop, my family files into my room like they're holding an intervention- four solemn faces all in a row.

Dad has gotten much older; I've noticed that since I've been back home. His skin has darkened with aging spots, his hair has grayed, and his belly has grown rounder.

I don't look much like either of my parents. If I had to pick the one I more closely resemble, it would be Dad because it's my grandma on his side that I actually look like. There are pictures from when she was young, brand new to America right after she left Korea. In those pictures, we look like we could be twins.

Dad always attributes my beauty to Mom's side of the family, but I'm not as soft as them.

That's how I know I'm my father's daughter.

June and Griffin got all of Mom. They're flawless; they never age. Forty-eight years haven't changed Mom at all. She's still beautiful, big-eyed, and even-mannered.

Dad always jokes about what a catch Mom is, how fortunate he is that he ended up with such a beautiful wife, inside and out.

Once, when Andy and I came back for Winter Break, Dad told him, "The fact that the Jeong girls pay attention to men like us is a blessing in itself."

Andy laughed and agreed.

"Who ever thought such beautiful women would be attracted to us?" Andy had said.

But I always felt honored that a guy like Andy was ever interested in me.

Tables have a funny way of turning.

Now it's just Dad who has a Jeong girl to call his own.

"Well, if this isn't an ambush..." I murmur, taking the headphones out of my ears. "Please don't do this right now."

"You need to talk to someone," Mom says.

I roll my eyes. They've been hinting at this all week. "Give me some time! I'm going through a breakup."

"This isn't about Andy," Dad says. It sounds rehearsed coming out of his mouth, and I know Mom trained him on what he should say.

It's not my breakup they're concerned about; it's everything that happened before. It's about the night Andy called them in the middle of the night, speaking in hushed tones so I wouldn't hear. It's about the months of spiraling leading up to that.

"Andy was worried about you too-"

"Yes, he was, but he didn't attack me like this," I retaliate.

Mom sits on my bed to make me feel more at ease. It doesn't work.

"We've already made the appointment," she informs me.

I throw my hands in the air. Almost twenty years old, and my mother still makes decisions for me. "Unbelievable. You don't *listen* to me. You don't even talk to me! You just go behind my back and think you know what's best for me. It's insane."

When did I become so combative, willing to argue with my family? Was it just something else I picked up from Andy in the long stream of traits I'd adopted from him? We'd grown together, adapting and changing our personalities until we became intertwined. Breaking apart from him left dangling strands of shared qualities neither of us knew who would take after the psychological divorce.

There are parts of him left in me still. I enjoy keeping some parts with me as a reminder that we'll always be connected in some cosmic way. But there are others attributes I wish he'd take back- one of them being his strained communication with his parents.

"You're staying with us," Mom points out. "And we're all concerned about your health."

"Really? *All* of you are concerned? Griffin is literally on his phone right now. He doesn't look concerned."

Griffin glares at me through the bangs that need to be trimmed. Dad takes away the phone, and Griffin sulks, crossing his skinny arms across his chest.

I resist the urge to stick out my tongue.

See, I do have an interest in normal activities. I still have the desire to fight with my siblings. I can't be too bad off.

"In his defense, Griffin's missing a party because Mom and Dad wanted him to be here for you. Somewhere in there, beneath all the annoyance, he's concerned," June offers.

Twelve-year-olds don't get concerned about their older sisters. Maybe some do, but not Griffin.

"Let her do what she wants," Griffin complains.

"I'll buy you a new video game just for that comment," I tell him.

He grins, and his smile takes up half his face.

"Rebecca, this isn't negotiable, and this isn't just about Andy. You know it's not."

The memories still sear my brain, and I wish Mom would stop reminding me.

"Yes, I'm aware," I snap, immediately regretting it when I see her face fall.

There's no getting out of it. Mom will insist on driving me to the appointment, and unless I hide out in the bathroom of the doctor's office for an hour, I'm going to have to go in and talk to the therapist. Mom won't let this go. Neither will Dad.

Neither will June.

At least Griffin's on my side.

"When's the appointment?" I ask.

"In an hour."

I scoff. "You're kidding."

"You'll think of some excuse if we give you too much time," Mom says.

She's not wrong.

"It'll be good for you," Dad says.

I roll my eyes. "I haven't even showered."

"That's part of the problem." Mom stands up. "I'll drive you over. Be ready in thirty minutes."

And with that, they leave my room, offering sympathetic smiles on their way out.

Griffin pops his head back into my room and says, "You really should hop in the shower. You smell worse than me."

I end up taking his advice.

I stand in the shower, letting the water run over me. My skin is sensitive, and I'm hyperaware of the way the steady stream touches my skin.

I dry off and stare at myself in the mirror a lot longer than I should. I know no good comes from examining every part of myself. But I can't help it. I inspect my reflection to see how much I've aged over the past two years, nearly berating myself for the change in the mirror.

Look at how dark my eyes have become.

See how my stress breakouts came back.

Look at how I've gained weight since I've been on my own.

Analyze every imperfection and try to figure out why it's there, why I let it be anything less than perfect, and why I went this long without fixing it.

When did I start looking so tired? Was it before he came along or after he left?

How did I let Andy Bynes, the well-known geek of the school, do this to me? How did I become so broken?

I pull on an oversized shirt and jeans, throw my wet hair into a bun, and Mom takes me to therapy.

. . .

Dr. Sherman is a 1940's wannabe, and somehow it works for her. Her short, gray hair curls in dramatic waves, and her lipstick is dark and pointed at the top. Smoke wrinkles mark the skin around her lips.

I already filled out the excessive paperwork in the waiting room, but she still reviews the final legalities while I nod.

Everything in here is confidential unless I express a desire to harm myself or someone else.

She is not here to judge me.

Her goal is to make me feel heard and respected.

"Is there anything you want to start with?" she asks.

I shake my head. "Not in particular."

She nods and looks down at her clipboard.

"Okay, then let's start with how your day is going."

"Pretty good. No complaints," I lie.

"Really?"

"*Really.*"

I don't usually act out. I don't disagree with people just for the fun of it. I wasn't raised that way, and if Mom were here, she'd smack me. But this was her choice to put me here. It was her choice to sign me up for these sessions twice a week for the rest of the summer.

"Your mother has expressed concerns about you being in a state of isolation."

"A mild state."

"Well, let's start with that."

I breathe out, but I don't say anything. I'm not ready to talk about what happened with Andy, what happened with school, what trauma I've experienced. I came home to get some rest, to get away from it all. Not to be forced into talking about it twice a week with a stranger.

"I'm sorry," I say. "I know you're trying to help, and I know I'm making your job ten times harder by being like this. I just don't feel comfortable talking about everything while I'm trying to process it myself."

"I'm here to make you feel safe and respected-"

"I don't feel safe and respected here. I feel ambushed by my family. And I don't want to talk. I'm fine."

Dr. Sherman doesn't seem phased. She flips through the paperwork I filled out, examining my symptoms.

"You've been having trouble getting out of bed?"

I'm reluctant, and for a long time, I sit in silence. But eventually, I answer her question.

"I've been staying in bed because I don't see a point in getting up."

"And why is that?" Dr. Sherman asks.

I look at my fingernails. I need to paint them.

"Because I'm not with him anymore. He was the one who kept me going for a long time," I say.

"Who's he?"

"Andy Bynes."

"And he is?"

"My ex-boyfriend."

I think that's the first time I've said that out loud.

Dr. Sherman doesn't take notes like I thought she would. I'm thankful for that.

"How long has it been since you two broke up?" she asks. She speaks conversationally. Not enough to put me at ease or make me want to be here, but it's something.

"About two weeks." I pause. "They're not giving me any time to figure things out on my own."

"'They' being your family?"

I nod.

"Maybe your family is concerned about a deeper trauma. Maybe they believe that if you overcome this, you can start dealing with the other problems you're struggling with. Have you ever had these symptoms before, when it wasn't related to a breakup?"

I move in my seat.

"Yes."

"When was that?"

"Late last year, things got really bad," I say. "But I don't want to talk about that. This isn't the same."

She doesn't put up a fight about it.

"Okay. Let's go back to Andy."

I wait for her to ask me a question, but she doesn't. She patiently waits for me to start the conversation, so I do. I don't want to tell her things, but the awkwardness is palpable.

"I met him about two years ago, in freshman year of college. We went to Boston University. He was studying aerospace engineering, and I was Pre-Med..."

I trail off, thinking of our story.

I zone out, a million flashbacks racing through my mind.

The dorm room and my tears.

Video games and champagne.

The distance that we could never make up.

We ended in tragedy.

"I can't do this," I say, standing up.

"We can talk about something else," Dr. Sherman offers, trying to stop me from leaving. "There's no pressure here."

I shake my head.

I knew it was too soon for all of this.

the voice of a past life

Dad and Mr. Bynes have been close ever since the first time they met. It turns out they both are obsessed with golf and bonded over it.

Now, every time there's a game on, they'll call each other to chat while they watch.

I don't know if it's all dads or what, but Dad always keeps his calls on speakerphone, so you can hear what he's talking about. It's like those older people in stores who answer calls and talk really loudly.

Maybe they like to show off that they have people to talk to.

Usually, it doesn't bother me much. But today, I can hear Mr. Bynes' voice loud and clear, coming out of the phone in the next room.

He's chuckling about a shot some player made.

I bet he's sitting at home, a bow tie around his thick neck, holding his stomach as he laughs. Andy's dad is like a big, rich teddy bear. He's always really nice to me, and I like how his cologne smells like vanilla.

The next thing I know, I'm tearing up.

The little things destroy me effortlessly.

I put my headphones in and turn my music all the way up to drown out the painful reminders.

saving the prince

There are so many times I want to call Andy throughout the day. Because, although I don't want to admit it, I need him.

I need him to talk me through my anxiety, those times when I want to scream, those times when I could curl up in my bed and never come out again. I need to tell him about the funny show I watched or the new exhibit on the pier.

There's always something I want to tell him.

But I won't let myself call him. I won't do it because it's not fair that he saves me every time I ask. It's not fair to keep dragging him through this even though we both know we're doomed.

I think about him having his own life, making new friends, and planning out all the places he will visit in Europe.

And then that makes me want to call him because I wonder how he's getting on without me.

Has he moved past it all? Does he spend the days wanting to call me too?

If he does, he's never made it past picking up his phone. But I can't blame him. I won't call him either.

I won't let him save me this time around.

We go back and forth, saving each other. When we first met, Andy needed someone to loosen him up, to protect him from all his insecurities. To help him deal with his parents. But then the tables turned, and it was him holding me up on my feet.

Now it's my turn to save him again, and the only way to do that is by letting him go.

. . .

I go into Dr. Sherman's office for my appointment.

I had no intention of going today, and I told Mom that. I told her if she was really concerned about me, she'd give me more time. Not forever. Just a few more weeks. But then came my need to talk to Andy. And when I couldn't, I could feel myself breaking apart.

There's no outlet for me. I don't have hobbies other than listening to music, which just feeds my self-pity. I try to watch movies with Griffin, but it reminds me of when Andy and I went to those movies. I try to go out with June, but I see him in everything I see.

In the stranger with dark curls who passes me in the aisle.

In the cheesecake I get when we go to dinner.

In the way June's optimism regarding love reminds me of all I've lost.

And I don't want to ruin her outlook on love. She's so positive, so excited to have a romance of her own. I don't want her to see me, locked in my room crying every day, thinking this is what happens when you let someone get close to you. She deserves better than to see that.

So, even though I vehemently insisted that I wouldn't be

going to therapy today, Mom didn't cancel the appointment just in case I changed my mind.

I head toward the front door.

"Where are you going?" Mom asks.

"Therapy," I say.

Mom grabs her keys and drives me, never asking why I decided to go after all. I tell her thank you, but I'm not sure she knows why.

the reverse

Dr. Sherman has new glasses today.

"Rebecca!" she says when she sees me step into her office. "I wasn't sure if you were going to make it today."

"I wasn't sure either."

She leans forward in her chair as I sit down on the turquoise couch.

"I want to apologize for the last session. I may have taken a more aggressive approach than I should have. We don't have to talk about anything you don't want to. Okay?"

"Okay."

I planned on coming here and telling her everything, just pouring out my heart because she was there to listen. But now that I'm here, there's a hesitation anchoring me to omission.

I let out a low breath.

Tell her. That's what you came here for.

"I was going through a really hard time," I say before I can stop myself. "I don't want to talk about that yet. But Andy was so kind and got me through the unimaginable."

She smiles. "He sounds wonderful."

What should I say next? Yes, he was wonderful, but that wasn't enough to keep us together? I screwed things up, and he screwed things up, and now we're both alone?

I'm sure she can see the panic in my face.

"What's wrong?"

"I want to tell you things. I do. But Andy and I didn't end off right, and I hate myself every day for it. I hate him too. I always thought we'd get our happily ever after, but I don't think we're the sort of people who end up happy. And I just wish we could go back to the way things were when we first met."

She looks at her notebook like she's trying to solve a puzzle.

"The beginning is happier than the end?"

I nod. We saved each other. Everything was so kind, so sweet in the beginning. I don't know how we got to where we are now. I want to remember Andy as the one who told me the stories of the constellations, the tales of Cassiopeia and Poseidon. I want to think of him as the guy who called comic books "graphic novels" and had a passion so fierce you couldn't help but be swept up in it too.

"If you need to remember the people you were at the beginning, then let's talk about that," she says. Dr. Sherman's voice is comforting. "Start with the first day you met him. Tell me all the things you want to remember about Andy and yourself, and we can stop whenever you'd like."

"You think that will work?" I ask. I'm desperate.

"I think you have a lot on your chest that you need to unburden yourself with," she says.

"I think you're right," I sigh.

"So maybe if we start with the simple part first, we can get you the peace you're looking for."

I remain silent, playing with the hem of my shirt.

Dr. Sherman continues. "Have you ever played 'Worst Case Scenario'?"

I shake my head.

"Okay. It's pretty self-explanatory. I give you a scenario, and you give me the-"

"-worst case?" I say.

She smiles. "Exactly. So, if you open up during this session, what's the worst that can happen?"

I chew on my lip.

"I could regress into an even worse state than I'm in now, making me have a psychotic breakdown that could render me physically and mentally impaired for the rest of my life until I die, completely alone."

"Wow."

I fake a smile.

"Go ahead then, Rebecca. And anything less than a psychotic breakdown will be a warm welcome."

"Okay," I say, still uneasy. "I'll start at the beginning."

PART 2: FRESHMAN YEAR

andy bynes
September 8

I went to Hazy's because when you felt overwhelmed by the pressure of college, you needed to be surrounded by soup. It was just that simple.

My roommate, Hillary, who finally stopped glaring at me through her dripping eyeliner, told me she was friends with a senior. According to her, all the cool upperclassmen went to Hazy's, the best low-key restaurant in Boston. Hillary came here with her band all the time.

I went there for the first time and immediately saw the appeal. As I opened the door, a little bell chimed like an elf's laugh, announcing my presence. The restaurant was small and cozy, the wooden walls giving the room a vintage vibe. The fairy lights hanging across the ceiling illuminated the room more than the rays of setting sun coming in through the window.

I walked up to the counter, scanning the menu for the daily special even though I already knew what I wanted.

Anytime I went to a soup shop, I got the same thing: tomato basil soup and a grilled cheese sandwich.

A boy stood at the counter.

It wasn't his dark curls or his bad posture that caught my attention.

It was the faded orchid tie-dye sweatshirt he wore under his apron.

I'd wanted that sweatshirt for two months, but I was trying to budget myself before I wound up drowning in unpaid student loans.

But that guy had it. And to be honest, he was pulling it off way better than I ever could.

"What can I get-" He cut off, looking up at me for the first time. "Hey, Beck!"

"Hey," I started instinctively. But then I trailed off. I didn't know his name.

"Andy," he filled in for me.

The confusion on my face was apparent. "Do we know each other?" He didn't look familiar at all.

"Heck yeah, we know each other! Well, I know you. We're not acquaintances or anything. It's more like I've seen you around. Actually, it's more like my roommate has seen you around. I think he hung out with you last week? 'Hang' being a loose term," he shrugged.

He talked fast, which was good for my sake, or else his ramblings would have taken up my whole day. I would never have gotten my soup.

"Who's your roommate?" I asked.

"Isaac Johnson."

"You're Isaac's roommate?"

As I spoke, he mouthed along, anticipating my response.

"It's only been two weeks, and I'm already getting that a lot," he said.

Isaac Johnson was drop-dead gorgeous, and within the first two days of college, all the girls set their sights on him. His dark, creamy skin and beautiful smile made every movement captivating.

Andy was right. Isaac came up to my friends and I the other day and hung out for a bit. I didn't get to know him that well, but he seemed nice enough.

And here was his roommate, Andy, a geek through and through. He was too pale to convince me that he didn't spend all his time inside playing video games, and anxious energy radiated from him as he tapped his fingers on the counter. He was a ball of nerves and enjoyed the sound of his voice too much to shut up voluntarily.

I couldn't imagine what he and Isaac talked about. I wondered if Isaac was friendly towards him. Isaac didn't strike me as the type of person to be nice to people that weren't in his social class, but maybe being roommates changed that.

As Andy and I stood there, thinking about how we were acquaintances of acquaintances, awkwardness thickened in the room. I took that as my cue to order.

"Alright, can I get tomato basil-"

"Real quick," he interrupted. "Can I ask you for a favor?"
I tilted my head.

"Real quick," Andy confirmed. "I have this project for Human Studies. I have to spend the day with three people, one from each category. Do you want to know the three categories?"

"Do I have a choice?" I smirked.

"Not really. The first category," Andy said, holding up a finger, "is a Hero. The second category is a Drama Queen- or King, depending on who you pick. And the third is a Wanderer. So, you see, I *have* to hang out with you for my project."

"Which category am I?" I asked.

He squinted. "Is that even a question? A Wanderer."

Out of the ones he listed off, a Wanderer was the one I wasn't. I'd always had my life planned, always been on the same path. Even in college, where everyone said I'd change and evolve, I was still the same. I was still hanging out with the girls who dressed to get guys' attention and the ones who didn't waste time thinking about school any more than necessary. I surrounded myself with the same type of people, and I studied the same programs. I knew my place in the world, and I remained steadfast.

Never once had I considered myself the wandering type.

"What even is a Wanderer?" I asked.

"The ones who are always searching for something they can't place their finger on." He shrugged. "They don't fit in."

He thought I didn't fit in?

I learned, early on, that you must match people's

perceptions of you if you want to succeed. To my parents, I was the one without any problems. They didn't need another daughter to worry about, not when one already had cancer. To my siblings, I was reliable because if I were anything less than that, I'd ruin our relationship. To my friends, I was entertaining and fun. Teenagers only like you when you're shiny and new, and my worst fear was becoming dull in their eyes. How I behaved around my Korean friends was different than how I acted around my other friends.

I spent my life calculating what people wanted from me to present myself in a way that would please them.

But maybe I wasn't doing enough to convince people.

"Plus, I'm becoming a social expert in this class. It has nothing to do with what career I'm trying to get into, but my counselor said it's supposed to help me be more well-rounded, and it will boost my GPA. I'm already learning a lot of things. So, being the intuitive social expert I've become, I'm able to spot wanderers from a mile away. They're the lost souls of the world. But don't fret. I'm the dog whisperer of Wanderers."

I raised an eyebrow. "Charming."

"Glad you think so," he said. "Do you have plans tonight?"

"Yeah, I do," I told him. I was supposed to hang out with the girls tonight. Zoey was having a party. Like it or not, college wasn't much different from high school. If you wanted to make a mark, you had to show up. Show up for people's expectations, and most importantly, show up to parties.

"A party?" Andy asked. He thought he had me all figured out, and it was annoying.

"No. I'm volunteering at a senior center," I said.

"You're lying," he said.

I smiled. "A Wanderer whisperer *and* a human lie detector. Impressive," I mocked, my words laced with sarcasm.

"Witty remarks and banter are my specialties," he said, shaking his head. "Sorry, the role's already taken."

I suppressed a groan.

"I really can't do it tonight," I said firmly.

"Please, please, please, please, please."

I'd like to say that he stopped talking at some point around the sixth "please", but he didn't. He just kept on going, repeating the same word until my impatience won out.

"Fine!" I exclaimed. "Just stop talking!"

Andy threw his hands in the air and smiled wide. "Thank you for your generous sacrifice." He bowed to me like royalty.

He should have smiled earlier; I would have said yes on the spot. How could I ever say no to that smile?

"I think we're going to be the best of friends," Andy said.

"You do?"

"Yeah. I think this is going to be a moment we look back on, four years from now, and go: That's where it all started. At that soup shop."

I opened my mouth to disagree, but something made me stop. Maybe Andy was right. Perhaps this would be the start of something great, a sort of friendship that changed us forever, hopefully for the better.

There were a million ways it could go. There was no telling what we'd turn out to be. We could never speak again after today, we could become friends and then phase each other out, or we could become undeniably connected. We could get to know each other and fall in love. We could have a love story they wrote about in songs and novels: the unpredictable pair who stayed together through thick and thin.

There was always a risk involved when you let someone into your life. There was a chance they'd be your kindred spirit. But there was also a chance they'd ruin your life.

But I guess you took the risk, hoping that all the good they brought would stay with you, even if they ruined your life in the end. You could only hope that, if things went south, you'd walk away knowing you'd change nothing, that you'd do it all over again to experience that kind of love and connection.

I thought about it just long enough to convince myself that it was true, that we'd be bound together for as long as we lived.

"Best friends," Andy repeated wistfully.

"I hope you're right, Andy," I said with a smile.

I hoped he was in my life forever.

human studies
September 8

I sat at the table in the middle of Hazy's, waiting for Andy to bring me my tomato basil soup and grilled cheese. It took longer than it should have, and I knew he was stalling so he'd be off the clock by the time he brought it to me.

Finally, he came around the corner. "Your evening meal is served, mademoiselle," he said, putting the tray of food in front of me. He took off his green apron and set it on the back of a nearby chair.

"Let's start with the basics. I need to get a general profile on you for my project."

"Can't you wait until I finish eating?" I complained, my mouth full of the delicious food. Hazy's was quickly becoming my new favorite restaurant.

"Where'd you grow up?" he asked, completely ignoring me.

I rolled my eyes. "California. Born and raised."

He slammed his hand on the table, and I was surprised at how loud the sound was. "You're kidding! I'm from California too."

"I'm going to take my soup and leave if you keep acting like this," I warned. Andy was overly excitable, hyper, and *way* too talkative.

"Sorry, sorry," he said, lowering his voice and slouching

in his chair. "I'm cool." He slid his hand through the air like a knife while he whistled.

Cool, not really. An idiot? Very much so.

"I grew up by Laguna. You can see the shore from our living room window," he said.

"I lived like, twenty minutes from there."

"This?" he said, gesturing between the two of us. "This is fate. I don't know if you believe in that sort of thing. I don't even know if I do. But if I did, this is it. I mean, what are the odds that both of us are from California, we come to Boston for school, and then you show up in the restaurant I work at, during the same time I'm looking for someone to be the subject of my report? That's fate right there."

I didn't believe in fate. But it was an extraordinary coincidence.

"Okay, what are you studying here?" he continued.

"I'm in Pre-Med. I want to be a pediatric doctor," I answered.

"Very cool." He was trying so hard to be calm. But he was just a natural nervous wreck.

"You seem tense," I commented.

Andy looked over at me, a hint of relief in his eyes for addressing the jittery elephant in the room.

"I am. I'm just- can I be honest with you for a minute?"

I nodded, and he leaned forward in his chair, hunched over.

"I went out on a huge limb to ask for your help on this

project. I mean, you're more Isaac's speed, and you can see that I'm not Isaac's speed." He paused, flustered. "I usually don't do stuff like this, asking a pretty girl to spend the day with me, so I'm kind of freaking out here."

Nervous laughter escaped his lips.

"I thought this was just how you always act," I said, taking another bite of grilled cheese.

"It is. It's just magnified right now."

That made me laugh. And then Andy laughed because he made me laugh.

This evening was going to be an awkward one.

"Have you ever tried ginseng tea?" I asked him.

Andy shook his head.

"When I finish my food, let's go back to my dorm room, and I'll get you some tea. Tea would do you some good," I smiled. "And you can ask me all the questions you need for your Human Studies thing. And we'll just hang, okay?"

He breathed out a sigh of relief.

"Tea would be great."

. . .

"What's up with the geek?" Hillary asked. We stood outside the dorm room while I explained why Andy was inside.

She crossed her arms across her strapless leather top. Her dark lipstick made her frown look even more pronounced.

"He's not a geek," I said defensively.

She scrunched up her face. "Oh, but he is."

I waved her off. "Andy's interviewing me for a project. Just let us have the dorm room for a few hours, and then he'll be gone."

Hillary was displeased. "He's weird."

"No, he's not."

But she cracked the door open, and there he was, sitting on my bed, looking intently at the tea as if something was floating in it. He made a "rawr!" noise and jumped back, pretending some monster leaped out and attacked him. He must have spilled a drop of tea because he made a *whoops* face and stopped.

"He's definitely weird," we said in unison, closing the door.

"He's going to be here for a few hours, and then you'll never have to see him again," I said.

"Promise?" she said cheerily, clipping back her bleach blonde hair.

She left, and I went back inside to sit next to Andy, grabbing my cup of tea from the bedside table.

"So, why don't you have any plans tonight?" I asked. "It's a Friday night."

"Because I'm here with you," he teased. "No, I'm just not the party type. I can't wait until we're all adults, and I'm not expected to dance against some random girl or play beer pong."

I nodded. "I feel that."

He looked at me. "Really? I thought Rebecca Dae would be all about that lifestyle."

I shrugged. "It has its appeals, sure. But I think there's a time and a place. I'm perfectly content staying in on the weekend and watching a movie or something. You know?"

I expected him to look away like he was bored. My high school boyfriends did that a lot, looking off like my words were tiring.

But Andy stared right at me, nodding for me to continue.

"My sister, June, had leukemia, and usually, I'd just curl up with her until she was asleep. I couldn't leave her if she didn't feel good. I did that once, went to a party when I knew she was having a hard time. And I felt so guilty, hanging out with drunk teenagers while she's throwing up because of chemo."

"Do you think that's made you more conscious of things going on outside of your friend group?" Andy asked.

"Maybe," I answered. "Don't get me wrong, I love talking about all the shallow things too, but sometimes I feel like my friends don't see the rest of it, how much more there is to life."

He jotted down everything I said on a notepad. His handwriting was messy.

"Do you ever want to do something unexpected? Like, try a new hobby or hang out with a new group of people?"

I smiled and elbowed his arm. "I'm hanging out with you, aren't I?"

He smiled back. God, that smile of his was breathtaking.

"What about you?" I asked. "Do you ever want to go down a different path than the one you're expected to follow?"

He took a sip of his tea. He paused, struggling to weed out all his racing thoughts and focus on one.

"No," he said decidedly. "I want to be an aerospace engineer. Nothing is going to change that."

"I like that," I smiled. Andy's determination was admirable. "What about people? Do you ever want to change who you hang out with?"

He tilted his head. "I don't think I hang out with enough people to answer that. I'm an only child, and I've always entertained myself. I wasn't that popular in school, so it's not like I had a big group back then. I just do my thing and go with it."

Andy seemed so wise. Neurotic definitely, but remarkably intelligent. He saw things differently than the rest of us. He watched me profoundly, observing more than what the eyes could see. I was a puzzle he was putting together.

So technical.

Never before had I been looked at like that. And I loved it.

Andy spent the next few hours asking me questions about my life and writing down my answers. I told him about my outlook on the world, what I thought about politics, and why I didn't want kids.

I wondered how many people knew those things about me. I never talked about things like that with any of my friends before.

And in a matter of hours, Andy uncovered all of that.

Everyone just viewed me as a pretty face. But Andy

listened to me intently, hanging on each word I spoke, and I found myself wanting to share everything with him.

He shared his life with me too. He discussed his childhood best friend, Claire, and how she was diagnosed with cancer recently. He spoke of his parents' neglect, the mansion he grew up in, and why he hates the letter v. All of it was fascinating, even the minor, insignificant details.

As I spent time with him, I realized he wasn't weird at all. He had some different interests than me, but he was a genius.

I didn't know if it was the tea or what, but he loosened up after a while.

And I smiled because I was special enough to see a side of him that most people didn't get to see.

disapproving eyes
September 11

Zoey ignored me for two days because I missed her party. She said I wasn't putting enough energy into our friendship.

After 48 hours, her silent treatment had reached an end, though, because she waved me over like everything was fine again.

"Hey, Rebecca," she said with a smile. "So, I saw you hanging out with that *guy* the other day. What's that about?"

I looked at her expectantly. "His name's Andy."

She laughed. "Girl, you're wasting time on people like him. Make ties with people who can help you succeed, not the ones who are gonna prevent you from getting ahead. You're getting too friendly with the liabilities."

"You do realize how pretentious that sounds, right?"

"Pretentious is a compliment in my book," she shrugged. "Anyway, there's a party at Mike's tonight, but...I'm sure you're probably busy with the geek."

I faked a smile. "No worries. I probably am."

Andy was across the way, lounging under the tree. I left Zoey and joined him.

fresh meat
September 17

Everyone said college was hard, but I always took their word with a grain of salt. People said high school would be challenging too, and I did just fine during those four years. I was confident in my ability to thrive in college.

But only a month into school, I felt overwhelmed.

I sat on my bed, my mind racing as I tried to herd all my energy into studying. My books lay beside me, open to pages I should have been reading. My notebooks were begging to be written in; my pens ached to be held. But I'd been neglecting them all week.

The assignments were piling up, and I could feel myself letting everyone down.

My teachers were giving me low grades, and they started looking at me pointedly when they mentioned upcoming assignments. It was obvious they were getting tired of me.

I groaned, glaring at the stack of Pre-Med terminology flashcards that refused to be memorized. I flipped through them until I was in tears and back at square one.

I was angry at myself for struggling.

I thought of the picture on the wall back home, the one of my grandmother and grandfather. It was the first picture taken of them in America. They were only nineteen when they arrived here, after going through hell to make it. They were my age, and they had a child, bills to pay, dreams to achieve.

In the picture, my grandmother was the spitting image of me. But she looked fearless like nothing could break her down.

She had traveled seas and faced persecution and unimaginable danger, but she was strong as ever.

Yet, I couldn't handle a few college classes. I was weak.

When I was a child, my grandmother used to tell me: "At the end of hardship comes happiness." But in her steely eyes, I saw the real meaning of the beloved phrase: *We traveled to an unfamiliar place. We had no money. No belongings. Just determination in our hearts and a baby strapped to our sides. All that at 19. And you have the nerve to complain about your life.*

I was a spoiled, privileged child who didn't work hard enough.

"Hey," Hillary said as she entered the room.

I wiped my tears so she wouldn't see me cry.

"Hey. Do you have practice tonight?" I asked, hoping she wouldn't notice the tremor in my voice.

Hillary was the drummer for a rock band, Palm Trees and Powerlines, so when she wasn't in class, she was practicing with the band at Dave's house. They had yet to book their first gig, but they had already created a solid setlist, with some songs that could give even my favorite bands a run for their money.

She flopped on her bed. "No," Hillary groaned. "Our bass player got stung by a bee, right on his hand. And he's allergic to bees, so his whole hand is swollen, and he's in the emergency room."

My eyes widened. "Will he be okay?"

Hillary shrugged. "He'll be fine. Our band won't be, though, if he keeps bailing on practice." She looked at the menagerie of school supplies beside me. "Studying hard or hardly studying?"

"The latter," I said. Tears leaped into my eyes despite my efforts to hold them back.

"Don't cry," she said affectionately. But she kept her distance. "School is lame anyway. In four years, all you're gonna have is a degree, which is great and all, but half the time, graduates can't get jobs anyway because companies want experience."

"Is that supposed to be encouraging?"

Hillary shrugged. "I'm just saying, don't let the jacked-up

education system get the satisfaction of making you cry. They're already taking all your money. They don't deserve your sadness too." She tucked her severely bleached hair behind her ear. "You want me to quiz you?"

"You don't mind?"

"It's not like I have anything better to do." She rolled her eyes, clearly irritated with the bass player and his swollen, bee-stung hand.

Hillary joined me on my bed, pushing away the piles of books and notebooks. She grabbed the stack of flashcards and flipped through them. "These are made-up words. No wonder you can't remember them." She paused thoughtfully before showing me the first one. "If you memorize all of these tonight, I'll buy you a new vinyl."

"That's okay. You don't-"

"When someone offers to buy you a vinyl, take them up on it."

That night, I made it through all my words in record time. It's amazing what a bribe can do for a struggling college student.

the beginning of xeno
October 8

I spotted Andy across the way, sitting down by a tree in

the middle of the courtyard, a book propped in his hand, and a yogurt cup resting on the ground beside him.

My friends waved me over to their spot at the bench, but I kept walking toward Andy. My friends didn't like him. They looked down on him like he was inferior, and it bothered me.

Zoey already cut me out of her life. It started with passive-aggressive comments that gradually became less passive (one especially aggressive comment involved a slur that I'll never forgive her for uttering) and quickly escalated to a screaming match at a party. Long story short, we vowed never to speak again.

Some of the other girls from Zoey's crew hadn't taken such a drastic stand against me. Still, I could feel them getting bored with me, getting tired of my distance, and they weren't fighting to keep me around. I didn't feel like fighting either.

There was something in my gut telling me to stay connected with the girls, the ones who would help me make a difference during my freshman year. But instead of joining them at their bench, I neared Andy. I didn't want to analyze the motives behind my actions; if I had wasted too much time doing so, I wouldn't have sat beside him that day.

"What are you reading?" I asked, joining Andy beneath the tree.

He looked up at me, his finger holding his place on the page. "The best book ever written!"

"That good, huh?"

"It's called Xeno Attack, and it's the *best* science fiction novel. Have you seriously never read it?" He looked at me, dumbfounded.

I shook my head, almost feeling guilty that I didn't know the fantastic book he talked about. "I've never even heard of it."

He watched me, slack-jawed.

I reached over, grabbed his yogurt cup, and took a spoonful. "Please enlighten me about this wonderful book that I, as a mere peasant, am unaware of."

Andy held up the book.

"This is Xeno Attack. It's a story that chronicles opposing planets in the galaxy. There are over four hundred well-developed alien races, and there's more than fifty-three planets-Beck, you *have* to read it. Nothing I say will do this novel justice. It's a masterpiece. Truly, the peak of science fiction."

I raised my eyebrows. "That's a bold statement."

"What science fiction books have you read? I promise Xeno Attack is better."

He was so confident that his book was the best, and just because of that, I wanted to come up with some book he'd never heard of that I could say was better than his. But nothing came to mind.

"I'm not a big reader," I said.

"You don't read science fiction, or you don't read in general?"

"In general. I'd rather just watch the movie."

He groaned. "If we're going to hang out, we need to change that."

There was a pause before he said "hanging out" like he didn't know how to define us. Like maybe he wanted to say we were more than just two people hanging out.

Andy continued. "I'm going to give you my copy of Xeno Attack, which is already a huge deal in itself because I never let anyone borrow my books. I don't even want anyone *touching* them because when I was in elementary school, this kid had cheese dust on his fingers, and it got all over my book. Disgusting."

That was fair. I wouldn't want people touching my albums with cheese dust fingers.

"So, I'm going to be generous and give you my precious copy. If you read it and don't like it, then I'll owe you a whole week of tomato basil soups."

"And grilled cheese sandwiches," I added.

"Fine. And grilled cheese sandwiches."

"*And* you have to listen to a whole album of my favorite band, Red Light."

Andy squinted his eyes and leaned closer to me. "You drive a hard bargain."

I smiled sweetly. "Take it or leave it."

I was begging him to take it.

"Fine. If you don't like it, you get a whole week of free tomato basil soups and grilled cheese sandwiches. And I have to listen to that band you love so much. Deal?"

Andy held out his hand for me to shake, and I did.

"Deal."

midnight texts
October 10

It was the middle of the night when I completed reading Xeno Attack. I almost didn't text Andy since it was past 2:30 am, but he'd said to text him when I finished, so I sent my message anyway.

I have finished the peak of science fiction. Please tell me there's a sequel. Or fifty more books in the series.

I laid the phone on my chest, waiting to see if he would reply. He was probably asleep. I probably wouldn't get a reply until morning.

My phone vibrated.

Andy was calling me.

I glanced over at Hillary, who was asleep on her bed. I didn't want to wake her, but she wouldn't hear me over the music blaring from her headphones anyway. She couldn't sleep without music playing.

I answered the call.

"What kind of ending was that, Andy?" I exclaimed.

"Wasn't it amazing?"

"It was a total cliffhanger!"

"But it was an amazing cliffhanger, right?" he asked. He was so hopeful I'd say yes.

I smiled. "Andy Bynes, you're right. The cliffhanger was amazing, and I'm dying to read the second book."

"Does this mean I won the deal?"

I rolled my eyes. "Yeah, that means you won."

I could feel him celebrating on the other line. "That's great because I'm at your door, and I brought you the second book."

"You're what?" I asked, sure I'd heard him wrong.

"Come to the door."

And sure enough, he was standing right there, holding a book in his hands. He looked like a child- a very tall child- donning pajama pants and a graphic tee.

Andy looked so soft in the darkness.

The phone lowered from my ear in shock.

"Were you just waiting for my call?"

"Honestly? Yeah. I've been waiting for two days," he laughed.

It made me laugh, too, because I think he was serious, which was just so ridiculous and cute that I couldn't help but laugh.

"Hold on, let me go get your book," I said, leaving him at the door to grab the first novel. I hid it behind my back when I returned. "There may be cheese dust fingerprints on some of the pages. I just got *so* hungry; I couldn't help myself." I shrugged and handed it over. As he took the book back into his care, he flipped through the pages, searching for snack remnants. "I'm kidding."

"You're hilarious," he said, rolling his eyes. "So, what was your favorite part?"

"The scene where Draven destroys the Hondu ship. Like, I could feel his pain. He's not really even the villain. He's just in pain."

I didn't realize how invested in the book I was, but I found myself wanting to rehash all the chapters with him.

"Right!" he agreed. "And Mabel was the same way. I mean, she was imprisoned her whole life, and they made her into a weapon. I'm not sure what they expected. She was justified in turning against them. The whole genocide thing went a tad overboard, but..."

I smiled.

"I could talk about this book for hours," Andy finished. "You're going to love the sequel."

He handed me the second book.

"Thanks for letting me borrow it. I was really hoping I'd hate it just to get my free food and to make you listen to Red Light, but I truly loved it," I said, holding the book to my chest.

"I'll listen to Red Light with you," he said.

I shook my head. "A deal is a deal."

"I'll listen to it anyway."

"You want to?" I asked dubiously.

"Yes." His gaze was strong, and he held me captive by his stare.

"But not right now," I said and immediately regretted it. I didn't want Andy to leave. I wanted to stay up until the sun rose, talking about Xeno Attack, and listening to Red Light, and making him listen extra carefully to the poetic lyrics.

But I'd already put an end to the night before it even had the chance to start, and Andy nodded his head, trying to cover up the disappointment.

"Yeah, of course. Not right now. It's so late. I'm going to pass out any minute. I had a long day today, so, yeah, I should go back to my room and get some sleep. Yeah, for sure."

"For sure," I said unwillingly. I wished I hadn't said anything.

loud thoughts
October 15

"Why do you listen to such loud music?" Andy asked, out of the blue. He eyed the band posters on the wall of my dorm room.

I shrugged. "Loud thoughts need to be drowned out by loud music."

He turned to look at me. "You have loud thoughts?"

"Don't you?"

Andy paused thoughtfully. "No, I don't think so."

I thought about the times June was in the hospital, and I spent my nights with headphones on, destroying my hearing and overloading my senses so I wouldn't have to think about my little sister dying. I thought about the times I felt so used by people that I sobbed to the songs until I was numb and empty enough not to feel the pain.

I looked away from him, concentrating on the pattern of my bedspread. "Everyone has loud thoughts. Some people are just better at managing them." I paused. "Loud music is the only thing that can out-scream them."

red light
October 16

I was with a few of the girls, walking the campus grounds on our way to the nearby smoothie bar.

Andy ran up to me, his jaw clenched and his eyes blazing.

I ignored the way Evelyn sighed beside me.

They were getting so tired of me.

"I need your help," Andy said, without so much as a greeting.

My friends eyed him, a stranger approaching their throne. He was a stranger coming to take me away, and they could sense where my loyalties lay. I wasn't even dating Andy, but I was already choosing him over them. I was already defending Andy when they pointed out his flaws to sway my feelings against him.

I nodded at Andy and adjusted the strap of my tote bag as it hung from my shoulder. I walked toward him, starting to leave the girls behind.

"I'll see you later," I said.

"Where are you going?" Evelyn asked.

I knew this was the final straw. If I walked off with him, there wouldn't be any remnants of the friend group that had been crumbling since the second week here. None of them would be my friends anymore, not even the ones who had put up with me for this long.

I didn't give them an answer; I just followed Andy, letting him lead me wherever he wanted to go.

"I think I need some loud music," he said, not even looking at me.

A smile appeared on my face, and I grabbed his hand while we walked. His long stride faltered at the touch, but he recovered quickly, grasping my hand tightly as we went to my car.

Andy sat in the passenger seat, his leg bouncing, everything about him burning with pent-up frustration. Andy wasn't the angry type, not from what I'd seen so far. He never really showed much of any emotion other than nervousness.

But he sat in my car, bugging out and in desperate need of an outlet.

I flipped through the playlists on my phone and selected: Yell Until You Die. It wasn't as clever as my other playlist titles, but it got the point across.

Putting the key in the ignition, I backed out of the school parking lot as the stereo blared Pavement by Red Light. They were my favorite band of all time, and I went to their concert every time they came to town.

We drove down the road until trees were the only thing on either side of us. The sky darkened, warning of rain this evening, which improved the aesthetic I was trying to create.

I glanced over at Andy, who'd remained silent the entire time. He didn't look much better than he did when he first came to me.

Rolling down the windows, I said, "You have to scream."

He turned his head and smirked. The wind blew his curls into a messy crown of angst. "You want me to scream?"

"Do you want to feel better or not?" He didn't respond. "I'm taking your silence as a yes."

I turned up the volume as loud as it could go and felt Andy wince beside me. With the music blaring, I screamed along, the words flying like daggers from my lips.

"*You've worn me down and lied to me. I'm tired of you and all your games. My empty heart and hollow tree, my broken compass, and my false fame,*" I sang, my lungs burning.

Andy watched me, wide-eyed and a bit concerned.

I turned to face him, my annoyance getting the better of me.

"Are you going to sing with me, or are you just going to sit there with that dumb look on your face?"

He rolled his eyes. "I don't know the words. You want

me to make up words to a song I've never heard?" He paused. "Hey, where are we going? I haven't seen another car in over ten minutes. If I had known you would kidnap me, I never would have asked for your help. I would have sulked in the library or complained to the janitor or something. It always worked before. It would have worked now. But no, I'm trapped in a car with a maniac taking me who knows where."

"You're impossible. Just scream," I shouted over the loud music.

"I'm not going to-"

"Andy. Do you trust me?"

"The person who won't tell me where we're going? Not really."

"We're *driving*. Why does there have to be a destination? Just trust me. Would you please yell?"

Andy rolled his eyes, but he yelled, his voice loud and booming through the air.

I kept driving down the isolated road, yelling along with him.

He was louder than I ever thought Andy could be. He out-screamed me, Red Light, and his inner demons. There was no way any thinking could be happening in his mind right then.

He leaned out the window like a puppy dog.

Three songs passed by the time Andy stopped screaming his head off. He settled back into the seat, out of breath and relieved, by the looks of it.

We didn't speak a word until we circled back and pulled

into the school parking lot.

The dark clouds had finally unleashed the rain, and the torrent poured on the windshield of my car.

"Can you send me that playlist?" he asked as we sat in the parked car, watching the raindrops roll down the windows.

"For sure."

He nodded. "And one more thing."

Andy leaned over and kissed me. It was sudden and a little sloppy in its intensity, but there was no denying that it happened.

I pulled away a few inches, putting a hand on his chest so I wouldn't be tempted to run it through his hair.

"Are you doing this because you're upset, or..." I asked.

His heart was racing. I could feel it beating through his sweater.

"No. I'm doing this because I've wanted to for a long time, and I don't have anything to lose."

I watched him for a moment. His eyes were clear, dead serious.

"Okay, then." And I pulled him to me again.

it's hardest for the kids
October 17

It was the middle of the night when I heard the knock. I

sleepily stumbled to the door, trying not to wake Hillary. The floor was cold against my bare feet.

Isaac, Andy's roommate, stood in the doorframe.

"Rebecca, he needs you."

That was all he had to say. I followed Isaac down the hall, dressed in pajama shorts and a tank top. When we reached their dorm room, Isaac let me in first.

Andy was sitting at the edge of the bed, his head in his hands. I knew that stance. It was the stance of someone who was letting the weight of the world crush them.

It hurt me to see him like that.

I sat beside him and wrapped an arm around his back.

"Do you want to talk about it?" I asked.

He lifted his head but didn't correct his stance. "It's so stupid," he laughed. "I'm eighteen, and I'm upset that my parents are getting divorced? Most kids have to deal with this when they're nine. And here I am, being a baby about it."

I shook my head. "It's still hard to watch people who used to love each other break up."

"But that's the thing. My parents never loved each other. My mom cheated on my dad all the time. We all knew it, but nobody ever talked about it. I just figured it would go on like that forever. But they were just waiting for me to move out. It was my dad's idea, I'm sure. We would have been better off without her, though. I don't know why he waited so long to divorce her."

I didn't think I could stay with a person who cheated on me, even if it was for the sake of a kid, like Andy.

"This sucks," he said.

He said it like a child, and I just wanted to hold him until he didn't feel bad anymore.

"I know," I said, resting my head on his shoulder. "I know."

the job hunt
October 19

Andy came by my dorm room to pick me up for our first official date. He planned to take me to a carnival and a fancy restaurant with caviar that cost more than entire meals. And, as much as I'd been looking forward to it all week, I got a call just before he arrived that sent me into a spiral.

A cafe called to say they had already hired someone for the position.

I'd gone on seven interviews in the past two weeks, and none of them hired me. Sometimes it was because I didn't have enough experience. Other times, it was because they'd found someone more qualified.

But the interview for the cafe went great, and I'd really believed I'd get the job.

When I saw they were calling me, I lunged for my phone and picked it up, my heart racing. I was so sure it was the cafe informing me of my hiring, but they only called to say I wasn't the right choice for the job.

"What's wrong?" Andy said as soon as he saw me. He came into the dorm room and closed the door behind him.

"That cafe," I said, nodding, "They just called about my interview. They're not going to hire me. I- *ugh*, I *really* thought I had that one. How do people get jobs? I've applied everywhere in the area that's hiring, and I'm just getting rejected left and right. It's insane!"

I was on the verge of tears. Angry, hurt tears because I was doing everything I could, and none of them liked me enough to give me a job. I missed being a kid when people helped you out because they understood you couldn't make it in the world alone and when they gave you something from the top shelf just because you asked for it.

Andy held my arms. "Beck, sit down. You're freaking out."

"I *know* I'm freaking out," I said, pulling away from him. "But I don't have money, and I need a job, and I can't get one, and why are college textbooks so *expensive*? It's insane! We can't afford all this in addition to tuition. It's not like we're billionaires! We're going to be paying money to this place until we *die*."

Andy shook his head, sitting on my bed. "You're going to find a great job, Beck. I know you are."

"Tell that to all the hiring managers!" I paused. "*You* have a job at Hazy's. How did you get one? You grew up rich. It's not like you have any job experience either."

As soon as I said it, I realized how rude that sounded. "I'm sorry, I didn't mean that."

He laughed, amused. "Actually, I've been working since I was sixteen. It gave me a reason to be out of the house after school, so I wouldn't have to deal with my psycho parents."

I groaned. "My parents should have forced me to get a job. This is what I get for having supportive parents."

I paced the open space in the room.

"Hey, listen to me," Andy said. "We'll stay home and go through the job listings all night. We'll go on our date another night, and we'll find you a job."

I shook my head, tears streaming down my face. I was acting like a child throwing a tantrum, but I was too far in to stop it. "No, I want to go on our date. Because I already have my makeup on, and my bra is on, and you look *really* nice in that shirt."

Andy grabbed ahold of my hand and pulled me closer to him, wiping away my tears. "We can go tomorrow night. It's okay." His voice was so soothing it made me cry more. "We're going to find you a great job, okay?"

I stood above him while he sat on my bed, and I played with the seam of his sweater so I wouldn't have to look him in the eye while I cried.

"There's a new record shop that opened like, two days ago," Andy said. "I was driving by, and they had a Now Hiring sign in their window. What better place for you to work than in a music store? It's perfect for you."

"You think they'll hire me?" I asked, excitement lighting me up.

"If they don't, they're the dumbest people in the world." He looked at me with such certainty in his voice that he entirely convinced me I was perfect for this job. "Let's go down there tonight. I'll drive you over there, and we can talk to them in person. You could show them your insane music knowledge, and they'll *have* to hire you. And seeing you look as good as you do right now can't hurt."

I shoved his shoulder and smiled.

"Come on, let's go," he said. He took my hand and led the way.

. . .

Ledger's Records was the perfect music shop. They had a massive variety of vinyl and CDs, ranging from the most famous bands to the most underrated. And, best of all, they were hiring.

"Are y'all looking for something specific?" asked the owner. He was in his mid-forties and wore a backward hat. A nine o'clock shadow darkened his face.

"She was looking to see if you have...Beck, what's the name of that band? We've been in tons of record stores, and no one has it." He nudged my elbow.

"The Pent Ups," I said, offering up the most obscure band I could think of.

"That's right," Andy went on. "She's always finding up-

and-coming bands. Beck has the best ear for them. It's her secret talent: discovering bands before they make it big. She can always flex and say she found them first."

The owner nodded. "I believe that! The Pent Ups is the most underrated band I've ever heard. They're incredible. What's your favorite song?"

"Blackjack," I said. "I'm obsessed with it."

"Great song," he agreed. "Yeah, we have their album right over here. Let me show you." He led us down an aisle and pointed at the CD. "Here you go. This one's even signed. I went to see them when they were performing at a bar in Seattle, and they gave us autographs."

I picked out the signed copy and held it close to my chest. "I've never been so jealous of Seattle locals," I said.

He nodded in agreement. "Anything else I can help you out with?"

"Yeah, your sign says you're hiring?" I asked, gesturing to the front window of the store.

"Yeah," he sighed. "Hardly anyone has responded to the job listings. My daughter and I are the only ones working here right now. It's hard running an indie record shop when everyone just gets their music online. Are you looking for a job?"

"I am, and I'd love to work here. There are very few things I love more than music, and I'm only saying that because my family would hate me if I chose music over them," I laughed.

He chuckled. "I respect that. Do you have a resume with you?"

"Yeah," I said, pulling it out of my bag and handing it over to him. While he read over it, Andy squeezed my arm and gave me a supportive glance. "I don't have much experience-"

"As far as I'm concerned, your taste in music is good enough for me," he said, and I breathed a sigh of relief. "You can start next week if you want."

"Are you serious?" I exclaimed, breaking out into a grin.

"If you want it, it's yours."

"Yes, I want it! Thank you so much, sir!" And then, realizing we hadn't formally introduced ourselves, I said, "My name's Rebecca."

"I'm Jamie Ledger."

We shook hands.

"Any ideas on how to market this place better? We're not getting the traction I thought we would," he said.

Jamie was asking for *my* ideas. My ideas on how to market music.

"Where do I begin?" I smiled. I told him all about the school's podcast and how Ledger's Records could appear on one of the episodes to appeal to the college students. I went on an entire rant, spewing my ideas to him, grateful that he was willing to listen.

When our conversation was over, I purchased the autographed album and left with Andy, grinning ear to ear.

As soon as we were out of Jamie's sight, Andy kissed me in celebration. "I *knew* you could do it!"

"You knew I could do it!" I exclaimed, smiling bigger

than ever. "Thank you for tonight, Andy." I wrapped my arms around his neck. "I couldn't have done it without you."

He kissed my cheek. "You could do anything you wanted, all by yourself. I'm just happy I get to be at your side while you conquer the world."

vigilantes
October 25

Andy and I lay on my bed, watching a movie as we dozed off. It was late at night, and the TV screen bathed the whole room in color. I saw the light of each scene through my closed eyelids.

Suddenly, the door burst open, making a *boom* as it hit the wall with force, startling me out of my sleepiness. I shot up from the mattress, and Andy did the same, placing himself between the intruder and me.

"Calm down, it's me," said the intruder. Hillary. I relaxed at the sound, and Andy sat back down on my bed, still on edge.

"Really, Hillary?" Andy rolled his eyes.

"Did you have to come in like that?" I scolded her, annoyed about my calm, relaxing night being interrupted.

"Yes, I'm running from the law." She shut the door behind her.

I rubbed my eyes. "*Right.*"

"No, seriously, look."

Irritated, I looked over at her, squinting to make out her silhouette in the TV light. There was an odd shape near her arm like she was carrying something.

"What is that?" I asked, standing up to turn on a light.

"A cat," Andy said, sneezing.

"Are you allergic?" Hillary asked.

Andy nodded.

"Dang it, Andy," she groaned. "I was going to ask if he could stay with you and Isaac."

"Where did you get that cat?" I asked, stepping closer to it. The cat was small and thin, with striped, gray fur. It had a pathetic, sad look to it, but as I reached out a hand to pet it, it hissed with ferocity.

"I stole him."

"You *stole* him?" Andy asked.

"According to the law," she said. "But really, I saved him. I saw him with his owner at a bus stop, and the owner hit him. The poor kitty was so scared. I couldn't let that mean old man keep him! It's animal abuse. So, I took him."

"That's illegal," Andy said, rubbing his face. "Congratulations, you're now a felon."

"He was being *abused*. If saving an innocent animal is illegal, then so be it."

"Tell that to the police when the owner files a report against you," he said.

"Your bleached hair and leather pants don't make for the

most subtle getaway," I reminded her.

"Well, I'm not taking him back," she said, snuggling with the cat who hated everyone but her. I never imagined Hillary being affectionate toward animals, but she held that cat with more care than she'd held anything in her life.

"Okay," I breathed out. "Where are you going to put him? They don't even allow us to have animals here."

Interrupting our conversation was a sharp knock on the door.

The three of us looked at each other, deer caught in headlights. A sickening feeling set over the room, and we knew, without a doubt, the person on the other side of the door was coming to take the cat away.

"I won't let them take you," Hillary whispered in the cat's ear.

"What are we going to do?" I asked, turning to Andy as if he had the answers to all my questions.

"Ask Hillary. She's the one with the big ideas."

"I was being a good Samaritan!" she defended.

The person knocked at the door again. "Hillary, open up. I know you're in there," a male's voice said- our Resident Advisor.

"Andy, take him out the window," Hillary said urgently, handing the cat to him.

"I'm allergic."

"Hold your breath."

"We're on the third floor!"

"There's a ledge." Hillary ushered him and the hissing cat out of the room through the window, ignoring Andy's protests.

"Hillary!" called the RA.

"I'm coming!" she yelled, closing the window on Andy and the stolen cat. "Act normal," she whispered to me as she answered the door.

"Hello, Mr. RA."

"My name's Jeff."

"What are you here for?" she asked, hand on her hip.

"An elderly man told me you stole his cat? He followed you here and promised not to press charges if you return his pet."

Hillary shrugged. "I have no idea what you're talking about."

Jeff the RA was dubious at best. I tried not to look him in the eye.

"Hillary, don't be difficult," he said, tired of her antics.

"What? I don't know what the man is talking about! I'm allergic to cats. Why would I steal one?"

Jeff the RA peered around the door to look at me. "Rebecca, you're telling me Hillary didn't come in this room with a cat two minutes ago?"

I was a terrible liar.

"She didn't," I said with a shrug.

"You swear she didn't?"

I tried to put on my best innocent face. "I promise."

We needed to wrap this up before the cat attacked Andy. Or before Andy fell off the ledge of the building.

"Then you won't mind if I come into your room?" Jeff the RA said to Hillary.

"Go right ahead," she said, full of attitude.

Don't act so confident, I wanted to tell her. *You're going to make it obvious.* But Jeff the RA didn't catch on to her cockiness, and he found no incriminating evidence in the room. He stepped back to the doorframe, skeptical but finding no proof that Hillary was the thief.

"If I find that cat here, I'm going to report you," Jeff the RA warned.

"Fair enough," Hillary said. "But I don't appreciate the accusation, Mr. RA. I hope we can move past this incident going forward."

She was laying it on thick. Jeff the RA faked a smile.

"I hope the man finds his cat," I called out.

"Thank you, Rebecca. Have a good night."

Hillary shut the door quickly as he left, and I ran to the window to let Andy and the cat back inside the dorm.

"Were you having a dinner party with him?" Andy complained as soon as I opened the window. "This cat is trying to murder me. Take him."

I took the cat from Andy, holding the animal away from me as it hissed and clawed at my hands.

"Come here, baby," Hillary said, saving me from the devil cat. The animal curled up to Hillary's chest as if it wasn't an evil kitty fixated on clawing us to death.

Andy tumbled through the window, sneezing and itching

his neck. "You're welcome, Hillary," he teased.

"I appreciate you both for being accomplices," Hillary said, acknowledging our assistance in the cat theft. "Now, we just need to find a place for him to go."

We spent the next two hours calling everyone in the area, asking if they would like a cat. Hillary had an intensive screening process and insisted that she wouldn't give the cat to anyone unless the cat liked them. Most of the nominees didn't appreciate the late phone call, and the rest didn't want a cat.

I called Ledger's Records in a last-ditch effort. Maybe Jamie was looking for a pet.

Jamie's daughter answered the phone.

"Hey, Millie," I said. "We came across an abandoned cat who's in desperate need of a home. Any chance you and your dad would be willing to take him in? He's the sweetest thing," I lied, looking over at the devil cat. It wasn't a complete lie; he *was* sweet with Hillary. It was a shame he couldn't stay with her.

"How much is he?" she asked.

"Free. We just want him to go to a good home."

"Seriously? I'm off work in ten minutes. Can I meet him?"

"Absolutely."

Just as promised, Millie showed up at our room as soon as her shift was over. Hillary held the cat, already suspicious of the person who might be coming to take her stolen pet away. But when Millie approached, the cat didn't hiss or bite or scratch. The cat was happy to feel Millie's loving touch, and within seconds of their interaction, we all knew the cat would go home with her.

Hillary said a long goodbye to the kitty and- while speaking to the cat- inadvertently confessed to Millie that the cat had been stolen, not abandoned. Thankfully, it heightened Millie's respect for Hillary and her love for the cat.

"I'll be good to him," Millie promised, cuddling the cat in her arms.

"I know," Hillary said begrudgingly. She sadly stepped away as Millie took the cat with her.

"Good riddance to the evil cat," Andy murmured. Hillary gave him a sharp glance.

"It's okay, Hillary," I assured. "You did the right thing. And Millie said you could visit whenever you want."

"Stupid Jeff the R.A. I hate him," she seethed. "It's his fault I can't keep the cat."

She took off her platform boots and sat on the bed. Her hard exterior didn't seem so hard anymore, not when she was about to break down over a cat.

"You're like a vigilante," Andy offered, trying to make peace with her. He leaned forward on his knees. "You just saved that cat- terrible and murderous as it was. 'Hillary the Vigilante: Animal Activist.' We're going to make a graphic novel for you."

Hillary faked annoyance, but you could tell she appreciated the support. It was sweet that Andy took an interest in her. Hillary was the closest thing to a best friend I had here in Boston, and I don't know what I'd do if she and Andy didn't get along.

"It's not like this will be the last time," he went on. "I can already picture it. You started with cats, but you'll branch out to dogs and then turtles and hermit crabs and guinea pigs. All animal abusers will fear your presence in the shadows."

We all laughed.

"I just might do it."

"I know you will, Hillary the Vigilante," I agreed.

the pretenders
November 1

I showed up at his dorm, dressed up in a cute little red dress, ready for a party.

"Ready to go?" I asked, coming in after I knocked on the door.

I saw Isaac first, observing himself in the mirror, perfecting his look.

And then I saw Andy hanging off the bed, reading a book. He was already in his pajama pants even though it was only eight-thirty.

"Why aren't you ready? We're supposed to be heading over there now," I said.

Andy looked over and sat up on his bed. "I'm not going tonight," he said like it was no big deal.

"What do you mean you're not going? You're supposed to be my date."

Did he not see the dress I wore? Any guy would be more than happy to be my date for tonight—apparently, any guy except my boyfriend.

"Why do you keep trying to make me go to parties with you? I don't like them," he said, fed up.

"I just think you'd have fun if you came out with us," I said. "Zoey and the girls aren't even going to be there."

I wasn't trying to push him into anything; I only wanted to help him broaden out. He was like a little old man who just stayed inside, eating ramen and watching quiz shows.

"Why would that be fun for me? Why do you want me to go to parties with people who make it obvious I don't fit in there? What's fun about that?"

"They're not all like that."

He rolled his eyes, and suddenly, I was mad with his attitude.

"You never make an effort," I said. "I hang out with you when it's just the two of us because you don't like big groups, which is fine. I get it. I'm losing friends because of that, which I'm not complaining about, but I'm sacrificing a lot here, and you're not even making the tiniest effort to do the things I want to do."

It came off my chest so easily, like I'd been dying to shed that weight.

"Then go with your friends, and I'll just sit here like your pathetic little charity case for the night," Andy retaliated.

He was insufferable.

"Fine," I said. "Isaac will be my date for the night."

Isaac turned around at the sound of his name. "Actually, I was gonna meet up with this girl-"

"You're going with me," I said. And that was the end of the conversation.

"Fine," Andy said. "Have a great time drinking and pretending to enjoy yourself. Real classy, Beck."

"Better than being alone."

He glared at me.

"Let's go, Isaac," I said.

Isaac played the part so well. Without hesitating, he threw his arm over my shoulder and walked me off.

Let Andy try to get that picture out of his head for the rest of the night.

. . .

After an hour, my skin glimmered with sweat, and I was a little more than buzzed. I shouldn't have come tonight. Andy was right. We all just pretended to have fun.

But none of it was fun.

Not without someone to share it with.

I found a corner with a bean bag chair, and I sat on it. More like collapsed on it, but let me keep some dignity.

I watched the people, and even though I was a part of

them, I was disassociated. I was with them, but not one of them.

Andy once called me a Wanderer. He picked up on it the first time we met.

Was it true? That I wasn't content where I was? That I was searching for a different group to fall into, a different person to be, a different path to pave? Maybe everyone could see it except for me.

Isaac glanced at me from across the room. He talked with a pretty blonde, but he excused himself and walked over to me.

There wasn't another bean bag chair, so Isaac just sat on the floor beside me, his back resting against the wall.

"What happened to the party girl?" he asked, tapping my leg.

"She's tired," I said. I didn't mean for it to sound sad.

"Want me to get you another drink?"

I shook my head and lifted the cup in my hand. "I've had a lot."

There was a pause.

"How do you do it?" I asked him. "Pretend to be the person everyone sets you up to be?"

Isaac looked at me with a curious look on his face like he didn't understand the question. "It's not pretending if it's who you are."

It made me feel a thousand miles away.

"You gotta chill with the existential crisis," he said, rubbing his face. "You got years to figure it out. You're gonna be just fine."

He didn't get it.

"I used to be so cool," I said absent-mindedly. "I thought I was cool here for the first two weeks. And now I'm the one who doesn't have a date, hardly has any friends, and hates her life."

Isaac sighed. "Two of those might be true, but...you do have a date."

I looked up to see Isaac gesturing to the doorway. Andy stood among the dancing bodies, looking awkward and uncomfortable, but there, nonetheless. He'd changed out of his pajama pants and even put on a nice black shirt just for the party.

"He comes around eventually," Isaac told me. "It takes him a bit, but he'll get it."

I smiled, and Isaac helped me stand up to go to Andy.

When Andy saw me, his face filled with relief. Seeing how I grounded him made me happy; one look at me and the stress washed off his face. I'd never been more proud of myself for just being there.

We made our way towards each other.

"You came," I said.

"Yeah." He scratched his neck. "I didn't want you over here without a date, looking as good as you do. I don't know how any guy could stay away from you. I don't know how I ever let you walk away from me in the first place. I want to be by your side, always."

I smiled. "Well, that's good because I want to be by your side too."

He waved off my comment. "Please, you didn't even miss

me."

"I can't get my mind off you," I frowned. "I would have gone back to your dorm, but I'm trying to prove a point."

"And what point is that?"

I paused. "I have no idea," I laughed.

I went to take another drink from my cup, but Andy stopped me.

"I think you've had enough for tonight," he said, nodding.

"I think you're right." My words were slurred.

He put my drink on the table and took my hand.

"Dance with me," I said.

"Okay," he smiled.

We stood in the middle of the party, my arms wrapped around his neck, his hands holding me up by the waist. We slow-danced even though no one was doing the same, and I was so happy he came, even though it wasn't his usual scene.

"Rebecca Dae and Andy Bynes, everybody!" Isaac hollered, holding up his drink. "The most unexpected couple here, but the best, without a doubt."

Everyone clapped, and Andy smiled, shying away from the attention.

I wanted to thank Isaac for showing Andy that he was welcome here, for showing Andy that he wasn't the outcast he thought he was. But I'd do that later. Instead, I looked up at Andy.

"See, they love you," I told him. "Just like I thought they

would."

"You should have brought me to parties earlier," he said.

"Don't even start," I laughed.

video chats
November 5

June had missed me a lot lately, so I texted her every chance I got. I kept her updated on everything: losing friends, making new ones, dating Andy. All of it.

And she checked up on me like my life was a soap opera.

I was at a restaurant with Hillary, Andy, and Isaac when June video-chatted with me.

"June Bug!" I answered.

"Am I interrupting?" she asked.

"Not at all!" Andy called out.

Her face was close to the camera, and her eyes lit up when she heard I wasn't alone.

"Is Andy with you?" she asked. I let my family meet him over the phone, and my sister had already taken to him. Griffin did, too, once he found out they both read comics.

I moved my phone so that she could see Andy and me simultaneously. Then I scanned around the table, showing her Hillary and Isaac.

"Good Lord, he's beautiful!" June exclaimed when she

saw Isaac.

"Thank you, gorgeous," he said. He winked at the camera, and I leaned over to smack his arm. He flirted with anyone who looked his way.

"I'll get your number from my sister," she said in between giggles.

"Oh, heck no," I said, moving the camera back to me. Now she'd only get to see my face. "What'd you call for?" I asked, taking a sip of my drink.

"For Winter Break, when you come to visit, we're planning to go to the lodge, right?" she asked.

We went to the lodge every winter. It was a Dae Family tradition, a sacred occasion that we kept no matter what chaos was happening in our lives. Mom and Dad took off work, and none of us made plans during Winter Break so we could all be together at the lodge.

"Count on it," I assured her.

"Cool. I can't wait." Then, a little louder, she called out, "You're going to love it, Andy! Their hot chocolate is the best in the world!"

People thought we were moving fast, with Andy already getting to know my family and everything, but it was the perfect pace for me. He was so good with June already, and I couldn't wait for them to meet in person.

I couldn't wait to meet his family.

I hoped they liked me as much as my family liked him.

meeting the parents
December 23

"They're going to love you," he assured me while we sat in the car parked outside Carlotta's house.

It was a mansion with gorgeous white walls and a long driveway. It was the sort of houses celebrities lived in, and- with Andy's intel- I discovered that A-list celebrities made up the majority of the Bynes' neighbors.

"They're going to love you," he insisted.

"No, they won't," I worried, putting my head in my hands. "People who live like this," I gestured at the mansion, "don't love people like me."

"I do," he said, watching me with certainty.

I gave him a dubious look.

Andy grabbed my hand. "Okay, my mom might just *tolerate* you, but my dad will love you for sure."

I laughed nervously, a relieved giggle mixed with pure panic.

"I'm feeling out of my league here," I said. I pressed my free hand against my flushed cheeks. I could feel the warmth burning through my skin, a tell-tale sign of my fluster.

He waved it off. "Are you kidding? It's me that's out of my league in this relationship. Besides, my parents are going to make yours look like angels."

When he said it, there was something dark in his tone, as if his parents were too terrible to discuss.

Last night, Andy met my parents, and it was the dream interaction, better than I had even hoped for. My family was big on hospitality, and they welcomed him to dinner with open arms. Dad didn't give him the glare he usually gave to my boyfriends.

But I knew tonight would not have the same warm, fuzzy feeling. Even if my family hated Andy, they would've made dinner pleasant. I had a feeling the Bynes wouldn't do the same.

I wanted to sit here with Andy in the car that was dark enough to hide our insecurities. I wanted to stay in this exact position, with him in the driver's seat and me riding shotgun because that alone convinced me he had everything under control and that life would be fine as long as I was with him.

"Be prepared to get the play-by-play of my parents' entire, messy divorce," he said. Carlotta insisted on Mr. Bynes coming to dinner with us so I wouldn't have to meet them separately, and I could only imagine how awkward this would be. Two newly divorced parents having dinner with their son's girlfriend they'd never met? It would be horrible.

"Just stay quiet, and they'll forget you're there." Andy glanced at my face and tried to compensate for the fear radiating from me. "If it gets too out of hand, we'll bail."

Bail? That wasn't an option, not in my mind. Never before had I so much as left a room without excusing myself, let alone leave a dinner party with my boyfriend's richer-than-rich parents!

Andy kissed my hand. "It'll be *fine*," he assured me.

We got out of the car and walked up to the giant, rounded doors. He rang the doorbell and kept an arm around my waist to remind me I wasn't alone.

"I meant to tell you, don't ask about the-" Andy started, but he was interrupted by the opening door.

What was I not supposed to ask about? I wanted to call a time-out or rewind the clock, so I could be better prepared on what topics were off-limits, but Carlotta was standing in front of me, and just like that, I was thrown head-first into the lion's den.

A woman trying too hard to stay young, dressed in a tight black dress, opened the door. Her lips were pursed, and her eyes looked like stone. She didn't even seem excited to see her son.

"Hey, Mom," Andy said.

"Hello, Andy," she smiled.

That was all there was- just formal hellos as if they were two colleagues in a business meeting instead of a mother and son reuniting after months apart.

"This is Rebecca," Andy introduced me.

I held out a hand for her to shake, but she gave a look that made me drop it back at my side.

"How are you?" she asked, not specifying if she was talking to me or Andy.

"Great, now that I'm here," I offered. "Your house is gorgeous!"

"Rebecca, there's one thing you should know about me. I don't enjoy kiss-ups."

"Mom," Andy said. "She's complimenting you. Please don't spend the whole night searching for reasons to dislike her."

I tried not to squirm as Carlotta scrutinized me with a withering glare, watching me over her pointed nose.

"Your father is at the table already," Carlotta said, stepping aside to let us in.

I stayed next to Andy, afraid that Carlotta would snatch me up if I strayed from him.

In the dining room, Mr. Bynes stood up and welcomed me with a smile and a handshake. He was a large man with a round belly, and his smile convinced me that he had a kind heart.

We sat down at the long banquet table that was too oversized for the four of us. The distance between us all was insurmountable.

On the plates, there was turkey with gravy drizzled over it. It looked delicious. Mr. Bynes started eating, so I assumed they didn't pray. I was in the clear to eat now.

Taking a bite, I exclaimed, "This is amazing! Would you mind sending over the recipe for the gravy? My dad is great at cooking the meat, but it's always dry."

It took me too long to realize that Andy was trying to signal for me to shut up.

Carlotta was staring at me with an annoyed expression on her face.

"This is a recipe from my grandmother, and it stays in the family," she said primly. "People are always asking me for recipes, and it's exhausting. And to think everyone has the nerve to ask about my grandmother's food in the first place! What happened to food being a tradition? This isn't charity here. We don't hand out recipe cards to everyone who asks for them."

"Must you go on this same rant every time we eat a meal?" Mr. Bynes asked her tiredly.

She put down her fork. "Yes."

Andy leaned forward in his chair and whispered like his parents couldn't hear him talk to me.

"This is what I was telling you *not* to ask about," he whispered.

"You didn't finish the sentence," I replied.

"Yes, I see the issue in that now."

"Andy, are you done talking over the table?" Carlotta said with expectant eyes.

He sat back in his chair and jabbed at his food like an upset child.

"Rebecca, what are you studying?" she asked.

"Pre-Med. I hope to be a doctor when I'm older," I answered.

Simple and to the point. I couldn't go wrong with that.

"That's wonderful," Mr. Bynes encouraged.

"It's been incredible so far. I love the class, and the professor is a woman who was an M.D. for twenty years, so it's cool to hear her experiences while she's teaching."

Mr. Bynes nodded, and Carlotta didn't say anything.

A win for me!

"And how is school for you?" Carlotta asked Andy.

"I love it. It's mostly my prerequisite classes right now, but Engineering is my favorite."

"What are your electives?" Mr. Bynes asked.

I wondered how long it had been since Andy last talked to his parents. Did they only talk about the divorce? I was surprised they didn't know what classes he was in. I called my family every week, and we talked about how school was going. I couldn't imagine having my parents not involved in my life.

"I'm taking Human Studies." He said it like a question. "Beck and I met because I had to do a project. So, we spent the whole day together, and I did a report and analysis on her personality."

I laughed. "Yeah, Andy wouldn't take no for an answer. I went into his restaurant, and he started asking me all these personal questions *while* I was trying to eat."

Mr. Bynes chuckled at that, but I noticed the way Carlotta looked.

She seemed upset that Andy was having a good time. It must have been hard seeing her son enjoy himself with others when he couldn't have any fun with her.

I wondered if that's why she took it out on everyone-because she'd pushed him away and didn't know how to get him back.

All she could do was push away everyone he loved too.

"So," Carlotta said to Andy. "Out of all the girls in Boston, you picked Rebecca. Who would have guessed?"

She said it so condescending, drinking her white wine

after she spoke.

Andy's head snapped toward her, and his jaw set. It was the same way he looked when he was sitting in my car after hearing about the divorce. So darkened, like his mood controlled the shadows on his face.

"You're impossible! You wonder why I chose to go to Boston, and it's because of this. It's because of *you*."

"I don't understand why you always overreact to everything I say. All I was saying is I'm surprised you chose Rebecca out of everyone." She turned to me. "No offense, sweetheart, but you seem so average."

Andy stood up from the table when he heard that. "First of all, you can't rate people! I don't know where you got it in your head that you can just put people on some like, scatter plot, and say, 'Oh, she's better than that person,' or some crap like that. You can't do that with people!"

Only Andy Bynes would use the term "scatter plot" in an argument.

"And second of all," he continued, talking right over Carlotta, who raised her voice as well. "Even if she *was* average on your stupid graph, which I'm not saying you are," he said, turning to me. "But even if you were, why does that matter, Mom? Everything is average. But you find that one person who looks at you like you're their whole world, and you become extraordinary! You're only average when you have no love in your life."

I could see where he was headed, and I winced.

"I feel bad for you, Mom. Because not even you could love someone like yourself."

Her face dropped.

The whole room went dead quiet.

If I ever talked to my parents like that, they would disown me. But something told me this was how the Bynes operated, yelling and fighting instead of opening up and confronting the issue head-on.

I wondered if all their fights were just miscommunications piling on top of each other. I wondered if their conversations were just a giant bowl of spaghetti, noodles of hate so entangled that they couldn't even sort it out themselves.

Carlotta sucked in a breath. "Good job, Rebecca. You've turned my son against me."

"You've done that all by yourself," Andy said. "And on that note, thank you for the wonderful dinner. I'll make sure *not* to ask for the recipe for that."

Andy walked around the table, clapping his father on the back until he got to my chair. He held out his hand for me to take.

I looked back and forth between the three of them like a puppy, not sure whose orders to obey. Would Andy really storm out like that? And take me with him, making me an enemy of Carlotta for good?

But I looked in Andy's eyes, and I trusted him fully. Wherever he went, I went.

So, I took his hand and stood up, walking out of the

room, my heart pounding. This was exhilarating!

And just like that, I knew there would be no mending things between Carlotta and me. She'd take out her grievances with Andy on me, and it wouldn't stop as long as we were together.

"Don't trip over those clown feet of yours, Rebecca," she called out. She was the type of person who needed the last word.

In her defense, my boots *did* look big on my feet.

"Sorry about that," Andy said in my ear. "I thought she'd at least be civil tonight. I don't know why. She's never civil. But I thought maybe just this once..."

We made it to the driveway when Mr. Bynes called out to us.

I turned around and saw him trailing after us.

"Rebecca, that didn't have anything to do with you," he assured me. "She's a raging maniac who never learned manners. That's half the reason we're not together anymore."

"It's true," Andy added. "She threw a vase at his head once."

Mr. Bynes ignored that comment. "It was a pleasure meeting you. Make sure he doesn't get in too much trouble."

"Very funny, Dad."

The thought of Andy getting into trouble made me smile.

"Nice to meet you," I said genuinely.

"See you at home, Dad." Andy was staying with his dad for Winter Break, not his mom.

Mr. Bynes nodded. "It was nice seeing you, Andy. Have a nice flight home, Rebecca."

I had planned to visit Mr. Bynes' home once more after returning from the lodge, but his goodbye seemed final.

When Andy and I got into his car, I asked, "Did he say goodbye because he doesn't want to see me again?"

"No," Andy said, starting up the car. "He treats every goodbye like it's going to be his last. He's always done that."

It was interesting to hear of his dad's idiosyncrasies.

I wanted to know everything about how Andy grew up. I wanted to know his dad's best golf score or if his dad even played golf. I wanted to know where his mom went to high school and if she baked dessert after dinner. I wanted to learn it all. I wanted to be a part of his life.

"I like learning about your family," I said. I hoped it would prompt him to tell me more.

"And I like being with yours," he said.

galaxies upon galaxies
December 28

I'd never been to Griffith Observatory before, but I loved it.

We passed meteorites from outer space, and Andy reached over to touch one.

He was so wonderfully awed by it all, and his excitement made me giddy.

We worked our way to the terrace, where we found ourselves overlooking Los Angeles. The sun had just set, and the purple haze had already faded to black. There was the famous Hollywood sign and all the city lights in the distance. It looked so pretty from up there.

"I used to come here almost every day after school. I'd just sit here, feeling like I was on top of the world. And once it gets dark and the stars start to shine, you can look through the giant telescopes and see the constellations."

Him talking about it was infectious, and he transported his joy to me.

"What made you love space so much?" I asked.

Andy leaned over the edge of the terrace, his forearms resting on the barriers. He lifted his head and looked at the pretty city.

"My mom used to take a lot of trips, and it would just be my dad and me most nights. He didn't know what to do with me. My dad's always been an old soul, so it's not like he was the type of person to go outside and play sports with me or anything. But he started making me get out of the house more when I was little. He told me all these legends of the stars, and I just fell in love with it."

He rubbed the back of his neck before continuing.

"When you're seven, everything seems all-consuming. Someone is mean to you at the playground, and it feels like the whole world hates you. You miss your mom, and it feels like you'll be alone for the rest of your life. You know? Kids live in extremes. They throw temper tantrums, or they love with all their heart. There are no in-betweens because they're so consumed with that one feeling. And when I'd go out there with my dad, it was like everything fell away. There was this indescribable sense of serenity. I could sit out there for hours, just looking up at the stars. And when you're gazing at galaxies, who has the time to worry about what Chad said at school or how you lost an hour of TV time?"

Suddenly, it was like I unlocked this new depth to him. I learned something new about him, and I felt special because he didn't tell this story to many people. It was something that connected me to him, and I was falling in love.

"Wow," I breathed out. "I was expecting you to say something like you were fascinated by aliens."

He laughed a deep chuckle that went all the way to his belly. "That too."

Watching him out here, I could see what he meant about feeling serene. A peace washed over us, and I didn't know if it was because Andy was in his element or if there was something genuinely tranquil that took over you when you respected nature. But either way, I was more peaceful than I'd ever been before.

Andy looked ahead, stars in his eyes, and I felt blessed that I was standing with him, watching his ethereal beauty firsthand.

He turned to me and caught me staring, but I didn't avert my eyes.

"What is it?" he smiled.

"You're just...really pretty."

"You're pretty too."

To a set of prying ears, we sounded awkward and inexperienced, but there was none of that between us. It was him and me and all the stars smiling at us. I'd never felt more sure of anything in my life. We had something unshakable, something that would never be torn apart.

"What about you? What made you want to study medicine?" he asked.

It was the same question I got asked years ago. In high school, I applied for this opportunity to shadow a nurse for the day. There was a group of us, students who were accepted to the event. We started in a conference room with a few doctors who explained the basics to us, teaching us how the hospital worked.

We were all dying to get our assigned nurse. But that wasn't until after lunch. They got us pizza, and we ate while waiting.

One doctor asked the question, *"What's your why?"*

One by one, we all answered. Most of us had a family member who was sick at one point or another. There were many sad stories, and I remembered how one girl said her sister died of cancer.

She was Korean, just like me. We had the same bone structure, eyes, lips, and cheeks, but her hair was cut much shorter than mine. For the entire day, the doctors and students confused us for each other, and even though part of it could be chalked up to racial generalization, the uncanny resemblance was evident.

I kept thinking about her story and how she lost her sister. I thought about all the times we had to rush June to the hospital because she was screaming that she felt like she was drowning. If we had gotten to the hospital five minutes later, June might have died.

Then my story would have been the same as my look-alike. Then I'd be telling *her* story while we sat at the table.

From then on, I looked at people, saw how similar I was to them, and freaked out. One mistake, one little change, and I'd be telling a different life story.

I felt bad that my doppelgänger was worse off than me.

Maybe if they'd gotten to the hospital five minutes sooner, her June would still be alive.

"My sister," I told Andy. "We spent a lot of time in hospitals with June, and I saw the difference those nurses made for her. They could make or break her day. I want to be able to do that for some kid."

"You'll be an amazing doctor someday. I know you will."

We walked around for a while and looked through the giant telescopes so he could point out all the constellations to me.

At one point, I saw him watching me.

And there we were again, in a whirlwind of eye contact

that made my heart flutter. He kissed me, which really made the butterflies go wild.

I started laughing when we pulled away.

"What is it?" he asked.

I waved a hand, trying to hide the smile on my face. "It's just...It's nice having a boy watch you when he could be watching all the stars instead."

My smile must have been as contagious as his enthusiasm because Andy broke into a silly grin that he covered with his hand.

"God, Beck. You got me smiling so hard."

And that was okay because he had me beaming too.

cheesecake tasters
December 28

We stopped by a restaurant on our way home from the observatory and ordered only off the cheesecake menu. Plates and plates of cheesecake slices crowded our table.

"S'mores flavor," Andy said in a hoity-toity accent. "Your rating please, madam?"

I licked the cream off my lips and proclaimed, "An 8.75."

Andy squinted his eyes. "You have to pick a number. Round up or down. It can't be in the middle."

"It's *so* not worthy of a nine! Are you kidding?"

He laughed hard, and I took a picture of him cracking up with all the half-eaten cheesecakes in front of him.

These were the moments I would remember a few years down the road when I reminisced about all the good times. But hopefully, we'd have good times in the future too.

That was when I still believed the future was something to look forward to.

"This is your new contact picture," I laughed, showing him the image.

"Laugh so I can take one of you," he joked.

I slid down in the booth, so only my face was peeking out over all the cheesecakes, and I faked a laugh until it developed into a real one.

"That's a keeper," Andy smiled.

nosocomephobia
December 28

When we returned from the observatory, we were still laughing as I pulled out the key to open the front door. I didn't even know what was funny anymore, or maybe it was that everything was funny now.

Finally, I got the lock open, and we both stumbled inside the house, expecting my family to be in the living room. June had a soap opera that she watched every Tuesday night, and we were obsessed with the drama. The new episode would be on in twelve minutes. She should have been sitting here in front of the TV, waiting. Griffin should have been eating his second dinner because that kid was always hungry.

We were going to start packing for the lodge tonight.

But no one was home.

"Hello!" I called out, but I knew I wouldn't get an answer in return. The house was empty.

And in my bones, I knew something was wrong.

I glanced over at the table by the door leading to the garage. The car keys were gone.

It had to be June.

"Something's wrong with June," I said frantically. I could feel the panic rising in my throat.

"Maybe they just went out for ice cream or something."

He wasn't listening. He didn't understand. "We don't go out for ice cream on Tuesdays. We buy it at the store in bulk and eat cups of it while we watch our shows."

He held his hands up in surrender, and it was only then that I realized how defensive I sounded. I would have laughed again, but the anxious ache in my chest made it difficult to be lighthearted.

I pulled out my phone to make sure I didn't miss any messages.

But there were no notifications from Mom or Dad or June.

There was only a text from Hillary telling me how her

second date went. It wasn't good, by the way. The guy took her to some sketchy club, and she was pretty sure she passed a guy who was packing heat. Also, the date asked about her feet. They wouldn't be going out again.

I called Mom.

Andy stepped closer to me so he could hear the conversation.

"What happened to her?" I asked before Mom could say a greeting. She wouldn't have bothered with one anyway.

"She's in the hospital." Mom had been crying. "The infection got worse." We took her to the doctor a few days ago when June didn't feel good. The doctor had said there was nothing to worry about, that it wasn't a severe infection, that June would be fine.

They said she'd be fine, I wanted to scream. But Mom didn't need me freaking out right now.

I breathed out low.

"What do they expect?"

"They hope she'll get better, but there's...there's no telling." Mom was trying so hard not to burst into tears.

I wanted to tell her it was okay to cry when she talked to me. It didn't scare me; it never did. It *did* make me angry, so angry that I could punch through a wall. But I didn't want her to hold back because of me.

I didn't say anything, though.

"Are you back home?" Mom asked me.

"Yeah."

Andy's cheek pressed against mine as he listened to the phone call. It was annoying, and I glanced at him out of the corner of my eyes, but I didn't tell him anything. It was nice having a guy try to listen to your phone calls out of concern, even if it was obnoxious and an invasion of familial privacy.

"How did your date go?"

"Mom, this is not our priority."

She was stalling.

"June didn't want me to interrupt your date," she said finally.

That's why they didn't call me. June didn't want to get in the way of my love life.

"How long have you been there?"

"An hour after you left."

They'd been there all evening. Hours passed, and not so much as a single text from any of them.

I felt like a traitor, enjoying my own blissful world with Andy while my sister was in a hospital bed. I hated that they felt the constant need to protect me, even though I was the oldest sibling and should have been the one protecting them.

"I'm on my way now," I said firmly. I was on my way to visit June and to yell at her for keeping this from me.

I hung up the phone and jammed it in my back pocket.

When I turned to Andy, his face twisted in uncertainty.

He said, "I know you're good with being in hospitals, and that's where your career is going to be, but hospitals freak me out. Like, if I see any blood, I *will* pass out. Right there in the hallway.

101

Just *boom.* Out," Andy said quickly. "I'm just warning you now."

I didn't know that. I knew Andy never entertained the idea of being a doctor or nurse, but I never knew why. I wondered if we'd ever get to the point where I knew everything about him, to the point where we knew each other's thoughts and were perfectly in sync.

"You don't have to come," I said. "It's not like we can do anything."

Andy shook his head a few times like he was trying to talk himself out of saying, "*Okay. I don't want to go to the hospital. See you later.*"

"No, it's fine," is what he actually said.

I raised my eyebrows because his voice came out high-pitched.

"I'm fine," he repeated in such a fake deep voice that I burst into laughter.

"Alright, I'll be on the lookout for any blood, so you don't faint on me," I said, grabbing his hand.

We locked up the house and headed to the car.

"So, is it just blood that freaks you out? What if you saw pus or discharge? Would that freak you out too?"

I looked over at him, and he made gagging faces.

"If someone came in with a big, oozing wound, dripping blood, how would you do?"

"Stop!" he pleaded. "I will die. I'll die on the spot."

I laughed again like everything was okay. Somehow, Andy made it feel like everything was.

my little alien
December 28

As soon as we arrived at the hospital, I ran into her room. Andy was right behind me, but they only let immediate family in.

Andy switched shifts watching Griffin so Dad could join us in the hospital room. Griffin was strong, he was, but he hated to see June like that. When she stayed in the hospital, he always crawled into my bed and cried himself to sleep.

We tried not to make him see more of her sick than he had to.

I rushed to June's bedside.

She looked so tiny in that hospital bed. She didn't look well, her skin was yellow, and she had raccoon eyes. But she gave me a half-smile as soon as she saw me.

I wrapped my arms around her and hugged her.

"You had me so worried," I said tenderly. And then, pulling away from her, I snapped, "And I can't believe you, making Mom wait so long to tell me!"

She looked up at me with a happy look on her face. Well, as happy as a person could look with an infection ravaging their body.

"Did you have a good date, though?" she asked.

"Yes."

103

"Then my plan worked." She tried to laugh maniacally, but she ended up in a coughing fit. I stroked her forehead as she settled back down, her face flushed.

Winter Break was going to end soon, but I couldn't leave her. Not when she looked so hopeless. I'd betray her if I left. I knew I'd be staying even after the break was over.

June looked so tired.

"Go to sleep, my little alien. Get some rest," I said, kissing her forehead.

When she first got chemo and shaved her head, she was in an alien phase. Her erasers were alien heads, she only watched sci-fi movies, and she searched for proof of extraterrestrials everywhere she went. So when Dad cut off all her hair, she was actually happy.

She went around convincing all her friends she was an alien in disguise.

I started calling her "my little alien" to make her happy. Even though aliens weren't her obsession anymore, she was still fond of the nickname.

June smiled when I said it. And then she fell asleep.

waiting rooms
December 28

"Thanks for being here," I said, nuzzling my head on

Andy's shoulder. My arm looped around his, our fingers intertwined. We'd been like that for hours.

Mom and Dad fell asleep in the chairs across from us. Mom never slept when June was in the hospital, and I wondered if having Andy there helped her feel more relaxed. Before, she always had two daughters to worry about when we were at the hospitals, but now it was like Andy was the one who had to worry about me. I hoped it took some of the burdens off her.

"I'll always be here," Andy said.

It was those promises that made me fall in love with him. Those reassurances that he wasn't going anywhere, that no force in the universe could break us apart.

I traced his arms with my finger. He was hardly ever in short sleeves, but I got cold in the hospital, so he let me borrow his sweater.

"You know, your veins are really hot," I said, drawing invisible lines across the blue marks.

"I'm glad you find my high blood pressure hot."

the chicken platter
January 2

June was getting better, and they thought she'd be out of the hospital tomorrow or the day after. But it had been a long few days, and Griffin was going insane.

It was his Winter Break, and he hated being stuck in the hospital. He and June were upset we didn't get to go to the lodge and play in the snow this winter.

I wanted to take Griffin somewhere away from the hospital, but June needed me, so it was hard to leave her.

I stood in the hallway, leaning up against the wall, two seconds away from breaking down.

You could always test your nerve in a time of extended crisis, and it turned out my nerves were weak. They weren't good at handling the pressure. I didn't know why I was trying to become a doctor; I wasn't cut out for it.

But I hoped that with practice, I'd be okay. Because I was so passionate about it, it hurt.

Andy pushed through the double doors in search of me. I told them I was getting snacks from the vending machine, but I'd been gone for too long.

It was sweet that he noticed.

"How are you?" he asked.

I nodded so I wouldn't have to say anything. I didn't trust myself not to break down in front of Andy. I didn't want to cry because then he'd feel bad, and I'd feel bad for *making* him feel bad, and it was just a never-ending cycle.

"I'm taking Griffin to the comic book store to get him out of here for a bit. Plus, it's Wednesday, so I want to check out the new ones they have," he said. "Do you want to come?"

I checked my watch so I wouldn't have to meet his eyes.

"No, I'm going to stay with June for a bit."

Mom hadn't left June's side, and it was obvious they both needed a break.

Andy nodded. "Okay. Do you need anything?"

I shook my head, but then I thought of June and Mom.

"Can you pick up lunch on the way back?"

He nodded. "Sure thing. Text me if anything else comes to mind, alright?"

"Thank you."

He paused before pulling me into a hug. "You're doing good, Beck." When I was in his arms, I was invincible, like there was a force field around me. He held me like that for a long time until Griffin joined us. Andy kissed my forehead before leaving with my brother.

I returned to June's room, where she and Mom worked on a puzzle.

The nurses brought in some crafts and activities to do while June stayed there. It was the joy of being in a pediatric unit.

"Andy's keeping Griffin busy for the day. When they come back, he's going to pick up lunch for all of us," I told them.

June hollered. "Is he taking requests? Because I'd kill for a fried chicken platter right now. With some gravy." She got chills just thinking about it.

I smiled. "That may be possible."

Mom was working intently on the puzzle, so she didn't even look up at me.

I walked to her side and sat on her lap. "Mom, you should go home for a bit. Take a shower, get some new clothes."

She shook her head. "No, I need to stay with June."

Her eyes darted over to June like if she looked away for even a second, something terrible would happen to her daughter.

"You've been saying that for five days."

"She needs me. I can't leave," Mom said, her thin eyebrows coming together.

"Um, hello!" June said, waving a hand at us. "Hi, right there. Mom, go home for a bit. Rebecca is here, and she can watch me. She's going to be bored out of her mind without her boyfriend around anyway."

"But we're not finished with the puzzle," Mom protested.

"Your eyes are getting tired. You've been looking at it too long. You need a break. Besides, I haven't gotten any time alone with Rebecca since the summer." She paused. "I'm okay, Mom."

Mom wasn't happy about it, but she grabbed her purse, kissed June on the forehead, and left the room, but not before giving me a firm look over her shoulder. *Take care of her.*

I nodded.

As soon as she left, June sighed. "I love her, but she's been glued to me, and I'm starting to go crazy."

I smiled. "That's because Mom loves you and doesn't want anything bad to happen."

"I know, I know. She's an amazing mother, and I'm so grateful to have her. But I'm in the hospital, and I don't feel good, and I'm allowed to be a little cranky."

She had a point.

"*Anyway*, you still haven't given me all the tea between you and Andy. Spill it, please! I'm dying for some drama."

"Being in the hospital isn't drama enough for you?" I asked incredulously.

June shook her head. "There are no cute boys here. Just once, I'd really like a tragic romance with a hospital patient. Maybe next time."

"Let's not plan for a next time."

She laughed. "Tell me all about Andy! Mom won't be gone for long, and I don't want to waste our time talking about this stupid place."

Per her request, I divulged everything there was to know about Andy and me. I told her about how we first met, how he always talked so sweetly, and about the observatory.

She knew most of the significant events in our relationship already, but seeing her face light up made me so happy. She just egged me on until we spent the whole morning and half the afternoon talking.

I didn't even notice the time until Andy texted me, asking what we wanted for food. I told him about June's craving for fried chicken, and he texted back: *Anything for the kid.*

I told June, and she blushed. She loved Andy.

The boys arrived a little later, bestowing gifts of food for us. Andy served the plate of fried chicken like a maitre d', one hand behind his back, bowing slightly.

"Your chicken platter is served, mademoiselle," he said with a crappy fake accent.

"Was that supposed to be French?" June asked skeptically.

I laughed. "Truly a disgrace."

Andy frowned. "Hey! Don't gang up on me. I brought you all the food. I even got extra cornbread."

"I take it back," June said, picking up her chicken with an eager look in her eyes. "I love you!"

She poured gravy all over her food and dug in like a starved lion.

"Give her food, and she'll worship you forever," I whispered to Andy, loud enough for June to hear.

June just rolled her eyes and kept stuffing her mouth.

I turned to Griffin, who had a chicken finger in one hand and a comic book in the other. There was a peaceful look on his face.

"How'd the comic book store go?" I asked Griffin.

He looked over at me and grinned. "It was the best day ever! Andy got me a bunch of comic books, and he started me on Xeno Offenders: World Apart."

"Arguably the best graphic novels from the Xeno universe," Andy added, his mouth unmannerly full.

"And he introduced me to this guy at the comic book store."

"A kid I went to high school with," Andy elaborated.

"We went to laser tag too, and Andy covered me, so I didn't get shot. That's what you call it when someone watches out for you. It's called covering."

Griffin beamed, and I was glad he got along with Andy. I wanted my family to like Andy as much as I did. I didn't want his relationship with my family to be like the relationship I had with Carlotta. I wanted Andy to be a part of my family.

"Andy, we should go see that new superhero movie that just came out," Griffin said.

"I offered to take you to that, and you said no," I reminded him.

Griffin rolled his eyes. "Yeah, but now Andy's here."

"Wow, nice to see where your loyalties lie," I said enviously. "What about you, June? Whose side are you on?"

She scrunched up her face thoughtfully. "Team Andy for now, but that's just because he brought me chicken and cornbread."

She smiled at him, and he winked at her.

"You are the worst siblings ever," I teased. "No backbone at all. Won't even choose your own sister."

I pretended to pout, and Andy reached over, grabbing me around the waist and pulling me to him. I screamed because he tickled me, and then I was on his lap trying to slap his arms away.

We were all laughing, arguing, and being louder than we should have been at a hospital, but at least it made June happy.

Mom walked in when we were all in a hysterical frenzy. Everything was funny all at once, and the harder we tried to stop laughing, the more we giggled. Our giddiness was contagious, and even Mom broke into a smile.

"You brought all this cornbread for me?" Mom asked,

grabbing the whole platter from us.

We all shrieked and tried to get it back from her.

I'd never had so much fun at a hospital.

Who knew fried chicken and cornbread could soothe so many souls?

strawberry love
January 6

June was out of the hospital, and even though she felt better, she was still weak.

Unfortunately, Mom came down with something she caught from the hospital, so she stayed in her room to keep June out of harm's way. June's immune system was so weak, none of us wanted to jeopardize her.

I sat in the living room with June, who rested on the couch, a lap desk placed over her legs as she worked on a new project to keep her mind busy.

"What are you doing over there, June Bug?" I asked, looking up from my phone.

"Making Andy a friendship bracelet."

She was fifteen but still a child at heart.

"I want to thank him for being so good to us at the hospital," she continued. "He told Dad that strawberries are his favorite fruit, and I saw this pattern for a strawberry bracelet, so

I'm trying it out. You think he'll like it?"

I smiled. "He'll love it."

And he would because it was from her.

the extension
January 7

Andy and I should have been leaving for Boston, but I couldn't abandon June and Mom. Mom couldn't watch her while she was sick, and Dad worked during the day.

I called Andy before he'd be on his way to pick me up for the airport.

When he answered, I said, "I can't go to Boston yet. I need to stay here an extra week and make sure they'll be okay."

"Are they worse?"

"No, but they're not better yet either."

"Okay," he said. "I'll still come by to see you before I leave."

"See you in a bit," I said.

He was coming to see me before he left. He didn't have to, but he was. I felt like I was back in high school, where I'd gush about everything, smiling because of every little thing a boy did. He was so thoughtful, so sweet, and best of all, he was mine.

someone to call home
January 16

Andy was waiting for me at the baggage carousel when I landed in Boston. He had a cute little sign in his hands that had my name written sloppily on it. It was a tiny piece of paper like he didn't know where the actual cardstock was, so he just grabbed a grocery store notepad page. But it was the thought that counted.

"Hey, babe," I said, wrapping my arms around his neck.

"Hi," he kissed me. "Do you like the sign?"

"Very much. I especially like how quaint it is."

He laughed. "Without the little post-it note, how were you ever going to know I was here for you? You'd be wandering in the airport forever."

"Ah," I smiled. "Thank you for not letting me wander around lost."

The air felt different in Boston, and I loved it. I liked the style of people and how I felt different when I was on this side of the country, even though it was probably just the placebo effect.

I stretched out my arms and sighed.

"It's good to be-" I cut off before I said home. Boston wasn't home for me. It wasn't where I grew up, and it wasn't even where my heart was. I'd been there for less than a year, so why was I calling it home?

Andy looked at me curiously, probably wondering why I cut off in the middle of a sentence.

But watching him, I realized why I almost called it home. It's because he was there. Boston was where we started.

And he was my home now.

"Back in Boston?" he finished for me.

I nodded. "Exactly."

I spotted my luggage. It was the red one with the heart patch sewn on it. Andy went over to get it for me, and as he reached out, the sleeve of his sweater rolled up. I saw the bracelet he wore- the one June made him.

"You're wearing the friendship bracelet," I noted happily. June would have a field day when I told her.

"Of course, I am," he said. "It's trendy to wear friendship bracelets. I know you haven't been hanging out as much with the popular kids, so you probably don't know."

"So, you're my trend guide, now?" I teased.

"Yes, I am. And I am happy to report that friendship bracelets with fruit patterns are very cool. At least when your girlfriend's sister makes them."

"They're not cool, but they do make your girlfriend and her sister very happy, so thank you," I grinned.

It was nice having someone to call home.

the queen of the crowd
February 17

Hillary had been working on the laces to her neon platform boots for five minutes, and she was only halfway done.

"A girl's shoes are the most memorable thing about her!" Hillary explained to me. "I have to have the most memorable shoes out there."

"I'm pretty sure that's not true, but your shoe game is strong, so I respect it." I paused, watching her get ready. "Are you excited?" I asked. I'd never been in a band, but I could imagine how thrilling it was to perform in front of a crowd.

It was Palm Trees and Powerlines' first official concert at an actual venue, and we were all psyched.

Hillary shrugged. "It's cool, I guess."

She pretended she was indifferent to it all, that it was just *something* happening to her in the long stream of things that happened to her. But she was excited. Last night, I even saw her practicing her autograph in case a fan wanted it.

I made a mental note to ask for an autograph at the concert.

Andy came over to our dorm, and he was more nervous than usual.

I sat him down on the bed and rubbed his shoulders. This would be his first concert, and he was intimidated by the crowd. But he had a great plan: pretend he *wasn't* intimidated so they wouldn't sense his fear. That wasn't too far off from what the rest of us did.

"Andy, this is Hillary's band. You'll feel right at home. You've heard them a million times," I reminded him.

Hillary made us be a test audience when she wrote new songs. She asked for feedback even though she never took it. We knew every song like the back of our hands.

Isaac came over when Hillary was applying the final touches of her eye makeup.

Spotting her, he picked her up and swung her around like she was a little kid.

"I'm so proud of you!" he exclaimed. "Getting into a real venue? That's sick. Tonight's gonna be awesome."

Hillary slapped at his arm, and he put her down.

"You made me mess up my eyeliner!" she shouted, examining it in the mirror.

"Let me see," I said.

She turned to me, revealing a dark line on her left eye that went all the way to her temple.

"If you fill it in, though, it could be like a fashion statement," I suggested.

She turned it into a messy wing, dragging it out far from her eyes. Then she smudged it, so it streaked her cheeks.

"Better?"

I nodded, impressed at how easily she made a mistake look intentional.

The four of us paused in front of the mirror: Hillary, the

rock princess, and her trio of die-hard fans. We wore Palm Trees and Powerlines shirts that Hillary got from a custom t-shirt company. They'd be on sale for fans at the bar tonight.

"Blow them all away, Hillary," Isaac said, watching her in the mirror.

With that, we left for the concert.

. . .

We were three songs in, and I was singing along and headbanging.

Hillary was only the drummer, but everyone's eyes were on her. She acted up for the crowd.

The lead took advantage of that and walked over to her so Hillary would be spotlighted.

It was amazing how much she thrived in this environment. She always put on the front that she didn't like attention, that people weren't something to be craved. But when all the love was thrown at her and when she ruled the entire crowd, she ate it up.

At some point during the final chorus of the song, I realized Andy was gone. I paused momentarily, turning to search through the crowd.

I leaned toward Isaac, who was dancing up against some blonde. "Where'd Andy go?" I asked, yelling over the music.

He shrugged and then said, "Toward the back?"

I was too short to see over the crowd, so I started moving

through it. When I reached the back, there he was, up against the wall, away from the fans.

"There are so many people, and the music is so loud," Andy said. I couldn't hear what he said, but I could read his lips. He was dying to get out of there.

I took his hand in mine, kissed it, and led him out of the venue, where the fresh air greeted us.

We sat down in the parking lot until he calmed down, and his heart wasn't beating so fast.

"You can go back in," he told me.

I shook my head. "No, I'm here with you. Let's just wait out here."

From the parking lot, you could hear the music loud and clear, pulsing through the walls.

"I have an idea," I said, standing up and holding out my hand to help him up.

He watched me warily.

"Come on, let's dance. We can hear the music, and we already know the words. We'll have our own little concert out here. All the fun, without all the people."

He got up and moved awkwardly at first, but soon enough, he got the hang of the party spirit and screamed along to the words, jumping and headbanging to the music.

It was him and me alone in that moment, and time didn't exist. It was just us and the rush of excitement in the parking lot of a bar.

This is what youth was.

Finding those moments of fun through the pain. Finding the safety pin that would hold your heart together a little longer before it broke.

I wanted youth to last forever. I wanted that feeling to be infinite. And I truly believed that, for us, it would be.

video games
April 25

I never understood the appeal of video games, not when June got into playing them and not when Griffin started playing them.

But there was a new game that everyone was addicted to if they had the right console. Andy was obsessed with it.

Gamatchu.

Andy played Gamatchu non-stop. He hardly had time to eat or drink or finish his schoolwork, which meant he didn't have time to spend with me.

After a week of sitting in his dorm room while neither he nor Isaac said a word to me, I told Andy off.

"This is so stupid. You're wasting your time running around as a weird purple ninja, trying to kill those gorilla things and collect coins. What is the point of this? What even happens at the end?" I exclaimed, hands on my hips.

"You go to the next level," he explained, not taking his

eyes off the game.

"And when you get to the next level?"

"You just keep going until you hit level 125, and then you're done. But you can still go back and find little passageways and hidden gems that you didn't find the first time around."

Replaying the whole game to go through a secret passageway was too much.

"What level are you on?" I asked.

"87."

I stared at him. He was sitting on the floor, cross-legged right in front of the screen, eyes more focused than ever. His eyes were also more bloodshot than ever since he wouldn't sleep.

"Okay, so teach me," I said.

Isaac looked over at me. His beautiful eyelashes batted at me.

"Rebecca, you know I never mind when you visit," Isaac said. "But right now, there's a massive gorilla creature in front of me, and I need to concentrate."

He didn't think I was serious about learning.

"Andy, teach me."

His eyes glanced over to me before returning to the game. "You really want to learn?"

"Yes, and I want to be the best so I can help you pass all the levels and you can stop obsessing over this stupid game."

That was the real reason I wanted to learn. I wanted his attention for myself.

"Okay. Let us finish this, and then I'll walk you through

the beginning levels," Andy agreed.

. . .

Isaac wasn't happy about me taking over his controller, but Andy asked him to make snacks for the three of us, so he reluctantly left the room and let us be.

"Okay, you can jump with this. This is for speed running. That makes you spin kick. And that will move you forward," Andy explained, pointing to each button. "Up at the top, that's your power box. It has a recharge for your gun if you run out of lasers. Got it?" he asked.

"Got it."

Apparently, I didn't get it because we played the first (and easiest) level three times in a row, and I got killed by the gorilla things each time. The fourth time, I fell off the path and died in the ocean of acid.

But the fifth time was a charm.

I was able to pass the level without breaking a sweat.

I jumped up and hollered when the screen congratulated us on passing the level.

"Good job, babe," he said, but it was in a condescending tone like he was talking to a child.

I frowned. Now I was even more determined to be excellent at this game. Just to prove to him that I could do it.

We started the next level, and by the fourth, I had it. It turned out, if you spin kicked while you were powered up, you could kick the gorilla's molten spit back at him *and* recharge your laser ammo at the same time. I was getting good at that trick.

Andy glanced over at me while I did that, and I felt a surge of pride.

I could do this all night.

· · ·

We *did* do this all night. Once we got to level 10, Andy started jumping ahead so we could get back up to level 87.

We spent hours on it, taking turns and teaming up to defeat the angry gorilla things.

When it wasn't his turn, Isaac laid on the bed, watching us as he crunched too loudly on chips.

"Hey, how did you do that?" Isaac asked.

"Me?" I asked, pretending to be humble, even though I knew he was talking about me.

"If you run full speed and then use the copper power, you can kick off the walls," I informed him. Just a second ago, I was able to jump off the wall and land on the gorilla thingy's head to kill him.

I was very proud of myself for that one.

"Should have brought her in here earlier," Isaac mused. "Y'all already made it to 94, and you're in the harder levels now. It's been taking us twice as long. We'll be done in no time."

"No time" was roughly in the range of thirty hours later, give or take. We finally beat Gamatchu, the gorilla king, on the last level. Andy and I played that level, and pride surged through me when I helped them win.

The three of us burst into excitement, hugging, jumping, and celebrating. Isaac pulled out champagne from the mini-fridge, and we all drank.

"I have my boyfriend back!" I teased, hugging him.

But I was already missing the game. It turned out, I enjoyed shooting lasers at gorilla things.

"Want to play again for the hidden passages?"

Andy and Isaac both groaned and gave a resounding, "No!"

xeno con
May 3

We left before dawn to get to the comic con bright and early. Most of the panels Andy wanted to see didn't start until the afternoon, but he wanted to ensure we got the full experience.

It was a 3-hour drive, so I planned my playlist accordingly. I made it a little over seven hours, for there and back, plus a little wiggle room for any stops we made.

Andy handed me the aux cord as soon as we got into the car, and I smiled because he knew me so well.

I started up the music as we drove.

"Okay, so I have a few surprises for you on this trip,"

Andy said.

Surprises? I loved surprises.

"I looked up the best places to stop on a road trip and found this palace called Cow Belle, and it's a gift shop that only sells cow-themed products. They have udder earrings, cow stuffed animals, and an udder strainer, so when the water starts to drain..."

He trailed off as I made a face and shook my head.

"Well, you get the picture," he finished, smiling.

"Yeah, I wish I didn't." I pretended to gag. "Why are we going to the udder place?"

He dropped his mouth open, offended. "*Because* how often do you pass cow stores? Not very often, and I want to do things that I haven't done before on this trip." He paused. "Your other surprise is actually in the bag behind your seat. It'll make Cow Belle seem like a dream."

"What are you talking about?" I asked skeptically.

He focused on the road. He was pretending to be attentive, so he wouldn't have to meet my eye.

"Just look in the bag."

I turned in my seat and grabbed the bag he put behind my chair. I placed it in my lap and started rifling through it.

He had to be kidding.

"Uh-uh. You are deranged. Turn this car around right now," I said.

"I know, I know, but you're going to Xeno Con! You can't just wear jeans! You have to go all out!"

"Why can't I wear jeans, and you wear your outfit?" I complained.

"It's called a cosplay," he corrected.

I pulled the outfit out of the bag so I could see it in full. It was a dark green spandex suit, detailed in scales. There was a gold headpiece with lots of beads and delicate chains. The entire suit was covered in strings of jewelry, making the outfit glimmer in the sunlight.

"I'm not dressing up as some oversexualized snake," I told him.

"It's not a snake. She's an alien princess, and her name is Verulian."

"What book is she from? I've read the first five, and I've never heard of some weird snake princess."

Out of all the characters in Xeno Attack, he chose some obscure one I knew nothing about. Typical.

He rolled his eyes. "She's in book twelve. You'd know that if you'd read more."

I smacked him. "Hey, I read the first few books, and I liked them. I just don't see the point of spending all my free time reading other people's stories. When we're old, what are we going to say we did when we were young? Went to parties and had fun or sat at home and read?"

Andy turned to look at me. "Sat at home and read," he answered.

"Whatever, I'm still not wearing this thing."

"*Babe*," he pleaded.

I shook my head as he pulled over on the side of the road abruptly. Andy jumped out of the car and ran to my side. He swung open the door and dropped down to his knees.

"Come on, please! I'm out here in the middle of nowhere, down on my knees, quite literally- may I remind you- asking you to wear the cosplay for one day. For me."

He was utterly ridiculous. I didn't want to look at him because I'd cave the second he smiled. I'd do anything to keep that smile on his face.

That was the weird thing about being with Andy. I played hard to get, but I knew I'd always give him what he wanted. Because when he was happy, I was happy. I'd never felt that way with a boy before, basing my happiness on his. It was a feeling so strong that I didn't know if I should be touched by it or afraid of it.

"I'll give you back massages for a week," he started bargaining. When I didn't answer, he kept going. "For a month! And I'll go with you to the floating lanterns thing, even though I think it's an environment killer and too cliché, but we'll talk about that later. I'll even do the modeling shoot for your friend since I know she's looking for couples to add to her portfolio. Come on, Beck, isn't that enough?"

He was trying awfully hard.

"Fine," Andy continued. "In addition to all that, I'll also give you one free pass. Anything you want, no matter how annoying, or cheesy, or social it is, I'll do it. You get a free pass."

I stole a glance at him.

"Anything?" I asked. Andy liked technicalities; I didn't want any loopholes.

"Anything," he confirmed.

I nodded. "Okay, I'll wear the weird alien thing." He smiled. "Just so you know, I would have done it with just the month of back rubs. But I like how far you took it."

. . .

I'd never seen a more hectic place than a comic book expo. I thought the stupid alien costume Andy made me wear was over the top, but now that we were there, I realized he'd picked a relatively tame outfit for me.

I hadn't seen what he would be wearing for the day. He kept saying it was a surprise, so we'd change in the bathrooms inside. I was curious to see what cosplay he picked out for himself. Was it going to be a spandex suit too? Was it going to be as wild as some of the outfits I'd seen already?

There were people in full body paint, spandex suits with fur coats and cloaks, and futuristic fake weapons attached to belts, bikinis, and leather suits. And that was just in the parking lot.

"This is so exciting," Andy said with a thrill. He'd been buzzing ever since we stepped out of the car. He was bouncing back and forth, footwork like a boxer, the bag with our cosplays jiggling on his shoulder with every step.

"It's...something, that's for sure," I mused.

Andy wrapped an arm around me. "You love it. Don't even pretend like you're not psyched right now." He laughed and kissed the side of my head.

I didn't say anything because he was right. This wouldn't have been my pick as a destination, but maybe that's what made it so interesting.

We got inside and were surrounded by people who were all so fearless in what they wore. There were hundreds of people already forming lines, repping their favorite characters with pride as they took pictures with each other and talked together.

There was an entire community here, brought together by their love of one sci-fi universe. It was beautiful but also overwhelming.

"Why are you okay with these crowds?" I asked.

"I guess I feel connected to them somehow. Like we're friends even though I've never met them. Plus, I took like, three anxiety pills before we got out of the car, just in case." He smiled.

Andy found a nearby bathroom, and he handed me my outfit before going into the men's room to change. I went into the women's stall and started stripping off my skinny jeans and crop top.

The suit was difficult to get into. By the time I got situated in it properly, I was out of breath from tugging on the fabric. And then came the bodice and the golden headpiece. It looked like a candelabra balanced on my head.

Stepping out of the stall, I saw myself in the mirror. It almost surprised me how much I'd transformed. I felt like the alien princess, not some poser.

Was I supposed to put my hair up or down? I opted to leave it down, and I walked out of the bathroom to join Andy.

I placed a hand over my mouth when I saw him.

He wore the same snake- excuse me, alien- skin bodysuit, but almost all of it was covered by shields and armor. He had swirly antler-type spikes coming from his back, and it fanned out in a dark sphere around his head.

He lifted his arms and spun around for me to see better.

"Did you just color your eyebrows?" I said, stepping closer.

"If you'd read the twelfth book, you'd know I am the spy knight that's sent to gather information on Verulian. And the knights always have green hair because, during their initiation, they're put in a vat of Madium, which has lots of effects, but one of them is green hair, hence the eyebrows," Andy pointed out. "So anyway, the knight, Jammord, tries to get information to use against the princess, but they end up falling madly in love, and he joins her side."

I nodded along. A lot happened in the twelfth book. I wanted to read it when we got back to the dorms.

"I can see why you picked those characters then," I said, smiling.

"Yeah, that and because I knew you'd look super hot in it."

I held up my arms like those people on TV who were trying to sell something. "What, all this?"

We laughed as we walked around the convention. A few people asked to take pictures of us or with us, and even though Andy thought it was weird, I loved it. It made me feel like a celebrity.

Who knew you could get so much praise at Xeno Con?

If I had known I'd feel so glamorous, I would have started coming a long time ago.

champagne farewells
June 3

It was almost the last day of school, and we were all gathered in my dorm room to celebrate. Just me, Hillary, Andy, and Isaac. It had been the four of us all year. We were an odd quartet, but we got along incredibly well.

It was the last time we'd see Isaac for a long time. He was leaving Boston for good, returning to take care of his father, who had fallen ill. He was going home, transferring his credits in case he had time to attend college in Ohio.

"That's really selfless of you," I told Isaac encouragingly. "I'm sure your father is so proud to have a son like you."

Isaac shrugged gallantly. "That's what you do for family."

He was right. When it came to family, you dropped everything and helped. It was that simple, but simple didn't mean easy.

131

"Twelve more hours, and we will be finished with our finals," Hillary announced, her voice booming. She spoke as if she was speaking at a concert. "And do you know what that means?"

"No more school!" we shouted in unison.

Andy chimed in, "Until next year, but we don't have to think about that right now."

I slapped his arm, and we all groaned. "We don't think about sophomore year until August," I reminded him. "Right now, we think of summer."

Hillary hollered and popped open the champagne, making a huge mess. We all held out cups for her to fill.

"We've made it through midterms, and sexist professors, and terminology that makes zero sense, and endless essays," Hillary recounted. "And now, we are officially done with our first year of college."

It had been a long, stressful year, but we had come a long way since the first few weeks of school. I was finally getting a grip on Pre-Med, and my professor was even impressed by my work. I had gotten my first job, a job that I loved. I had stepped out of my comfort zone and found friends that didn't get tired of me as soon as someone new came along. I was with people who made me feel good. And I was *with* Andy Bynes.

Things couldn't get much better than that.

"And I'm touring with Felt for the summer!" Hillary added. Palm Trees and Powerlines had caught the attention of the rock band Felt and became their opening act. It was a three-month contract, and the bands would travel across the country, performing in nearly every major city. We threw a party for the band at Ledger's Records when Hillary first heard the news.

"And we're *so* proud of you!" I exclaimed.

We gathered around, joking and reminiscing about the year.

"You're going to forget about me the moment I'm gone," Isaac joked after a few hours had passed. But it didn't sound like he was kidding.

"That's not true," Andy disagreed, clapping him on the back. "Come on, bring it in," Andy said, pulling Isaac into a hug. His drink sloshed around and spilled on Isaac's shoulder, but Isaac didn't seem to mind.

Hillary and I joined the hug.

"You can't get rid of us that easily, Johnson," Hillary teased.

I was the last to pull away from the hug. I savored it for as long as possible, memorizing how it felt to have all their arms wrapped around me. Because no matter what we told Isaac, no matter how much we promised we'd keep in touch forever, I knew that was a promise we'd have to break. I knew we wouldn't stay friends...we'd be lucky if we spoke to him once a year.

I could feel Isaac slipping away, and along with him went my freshman year of college.

I tried not to think about the ache in my chest, and I drank champagne until I couldn't feel it anymore. When I got too drunk, Andy tucked me into bed, and Isaac kissed my forehead when he left.

Isaac was leaving, and I felt like I was abandoning him.

But even if we never talked again, I'd always think fondly of Isaac, the gorgeous guy with a heart of gold.

I hoped he'd think fondly of us too.

the clock that skips time
June 4

My first year of college was over, just like that.

Everyone said it would go by fast, and I didn't believe them. Years took forever; they weren't something that just passed by without you knowing it.

But this year was different.

It was a whirlwind that sped by. Like when you'd fall asleep on a road trip, and someone had to wake you up when you got there because you'd slept the whole time. That's what it felt like.

A whole year was gone, and I felt like I missed it, even though I was there for every second.

Before I knew it, college would be over, a whole four years of my life in the past. It was wild to think about.

I was so unprepared for the next chapter of my life. I'd focused so much on college that I hadn't thought about what would happen when I was off at medical school for another four years without any of the friends I already had.

It was scary to think I'd be starting over so soon.

But as long as I was with Andy, it would be okay.

PART 3: SUMMER

summer lovin'
June 20

If you saw Andy's insanely large sweater collection, you'd have never known he was from the West Coast. But now that we were back in California for the summer, his beach bum tendencies were apparent.

He abandoned his sweater wardrobe and donned board shorts and a loose pi shirt. Not the food pie. The number.

"Do you like my shirt?" he asked when he pulled up to my house.

I gave it a good look as I got into the passenger seat. He looked so proud of his shirt.

"It's a good thing you stuck to sweaters back in Boston. But don't worry, I love your weird pi shirt."

"And I love the weird shark shorts that you insist on wearing all summer." He faked a smile.

I looked down at my shorts. They were high-waisted cut-off jeans that had a little cartoon shark coming out of the pocket.

There were a few other shark patches sewn on in different spots too.

"*Hey*," I pouted. "Sharkie is cute. You're going to hurt his feelings."

"And somehow, you're more popular than me."

"Just take me to the beach, okay?"

He laughed and drove away from my house. Immediately, I put in my aux cord and played some music. The beach was only a twenty-minute drive, but I always put music on when we were in the car. I hung my arm out the window, feeling the wind on my skin.

I forgot what it was like not to wear a sweater all the time. Even spring on the East Coast was too cold for me.

"Time to show Sharkie to the real fish," Andy joked, giving me a surfboard when we pulled up to the beach.

I'd lived in California my entire life, but I'd never attempted surfing. Usually, when I visited the beach, I hardly even went inside the ocean. Andy thought that was pure lunacy, so he brought me down here to teach me.

We went to the shore, and he showed me how to stand up on the board. Andy listed off instructions for me to follow, most of which I knew I'd forget by the time I was actually out in the waves. It was like learning to drive a car. In theory, it was easy, but once you started doing it, it was a lot harder.

After a few on-land practice runs, Andy thought I was ready to go in the water. I took off my shorts hesitantly like I was worried the sharks wouldn't view me as an ally if Sharkie wasn't waving to them from my pocket.

"If a shark eats me, the blood in the water is going to be on your hands," I warned Andy with a pointed finger.

"You realize you're more likely to be killed by a champagne cork than you are by a shark attack?" Andy pointed out.

I waved him off.

We waded into the water, and I squealed as the cold water hit my stomach. I didn't know how lifeguards did it, jumping into the freezing water without hesitation.

"You're going to have to come in farther than that," Andy laughed.

I swam farther out to join him. The ocean seemed stronger here, more powerful than in the parts June and I used to play in. I usually stuck to the main beach, where all the little kids stayed. But here, the waves were different, scarier.

Part of me wanted to call it quits. Swim back, put on my shark shorts, and head to the main beach to make sandcastles and eat ice cream. But then I saw how happy Andy was out there, and I knew I'd stick it out.

"Are you good, Roo?" Andy asked, a shimmer of worry across his pretty face.

"Roo?" I asked.

"You know, for Rookie. Yeah, I like that. I'm going to use it more often."

"That's so dumb," I laughed.

"Nope. You're Roo now. Simple as that. And you can

call me Grand Surf Master."

"You're a moron."

"I know, Roo."

We were in deep water; I had to fight to keep myself afloat. The surfboard helped hold me up, but it was still a struggle.

"All good," I called back, raising my hand so he could see my thumbs up.

Andy swam closer to me so he could walk me through the steps again. "Wait for the right set, and then paddle. Keep the nose level. And then when you feel that extra push, that's when you stand."

The push? That didn't sound very specific.

We waited out there until a wave came that I felt comfortable with. Andy cheered me on while I paddled. The swell got bigger, and I felt that extra push he was talking about. I tried to stand and...

I tumbled.

My nose stung, water flooding my sinuses.

It took me a little bit to get back to Andy after I got to shore, but eventually, I reached him again.

"You were so close! The first time I tried, I didn't even get up on my knees before falling off." He paused, droplets of the ocean clinging to his lashes. "Okay, catch your breath for a minute and go again. You got it this time."

I believed him.

So I tried again, and just like he promised, I got up on my

feet. I stood up straight and pumped my hands in the air. I could hear Andy cheering over the crash of the waves, and I smiled. He said I could do it.

. . .

We stayed on the shore during the sunset, watching the sky assemble itself into a vibrant portrait just for us.

My back was leaning up against his chest, and his arms wrapped around me. It all felt so magical and safe. I could have stayed there forever with him, just listening to the waves and the chatter of other people who were enjoying the evening too.

"What are you thinking?" Andy asked me. His voice sounded so soft.

"Absolutely nothing," I smiled. "What about you?"

"You," he said. "I love you. I want to spend every day with you."

"Yeah?"

"Yeah."

"I love you too, Andy Bynes."

We stayed on the beach for a long time, and I was glad we were together for Summer Break. I couldn't imagine a better way to start the summer than cuddling on the beach, under all the pretty stars, with a guy who could tell me about every single one.

calishake
June 26

There was an ice cream parlor by my house called Calishake, and each month there was a different theme. June's theme was kawaii, which June was very excited about since that's the month she was named after, and kawaii was one of her favorite aesthetics.

So, when I told her that Andy and I were going there for a date, she begged to join us.

"June, no. This is a *date*, not a hang-out. No sisters allowed," I told her while I got ready. I wore a pink cloud pattern sweatshirt paired with a white pleated skirt and cotton candy socks.

It was funny how my closet ranged from leather and fishnets to pastel cardigans, but it came in handy for themed dates.

Andy was excited to go to Calishake, but he didn't have any clothes that matched the vibe, so I let him borrow an oversized pastel striped sweater I had. He would also wear the strawberry friendship bracelet June made for him, which I thought was sweet.

"But it's a *kawaii* theme, Rebecca!" she pleaded, dragging out her words for emphasis.

"And I don't care," I said in the same whiny tone.

"Fine," she said, storming out of the room. I almost

regretted not letting her join us because I knew she would channel her frustration into a plot that would make me sorry for saying no.

Andy arrived at 8:00 sharp. He looked so good as a kawaii soft boy. I never thought it would suit him, but it surprisingly did. He didn't look overly happy about the outfit I made him wear, but he wore it anyway.

I liked having a boyfriend I could do silly stuff with. The guys I went out with in high school were all too cool to do what I liked. They never wanted to go to rock concerts with me because that was too emo for them. They never wanted to have dinner with my family because we ate samgyetang instead of burgers.

They would *never* have taken me to an ice cream parlor dressed how Andy was.

But Andy didn't have a problem with any of that.

Part of it was because he knew he owed me for making me dress up at the Xeno Attack con. But he didn't even make me use my free pass from that day.

I was saving my free pass for when I *really* needed something from him.

No, it wasn't the free pass that made Andy oblige; he did so because he had a good heart. He had interests that most people thought were stupid, and he was grateful to anyone who gave them a shot. So, he'd do the same for other people's interests, even if he didn't understand them at first.

And I thought that was beautiful.

He said hi to my parents and made small talk with them

while we stood around, waiting to leave. Dad told Andy about a new sitcom that came out last week, and Andy said he'd visit to watch the latest episode with him.

Mom and Dad really took to Andy, which wasn't surprising because he was exactly the type of guy you wanted to bring home to your parents.

Mom didn't like how much he talked, but when he went on one of his rants, she was always amused by it, so I didn't think she minded too much.

"Go enjoy your date," Mom said, cutting Dad off before he could keep talking about shows.

I gave her a grateful glance as we left.

We made it to the driveway before I heard a little voice calling out to us.

I groaned and turned around.

"What do you want, June?" I asked.

I rolled my eyes when I saw her because she was dressed up in every kawaii piece she owned. She had her hair in pigtails, a round collar shirt under her pastel cardigan, and a purple plaid skirt. There were light pink platform heart shoes on her feet, and she even went so far as to change out her everyday blue oxygen tank bag with the one she custom ordered with an anime character on it.

Andy gasped when he saw her, and I put a hand up to his chest to stop him from running over to pinch her cheeks.

"Stop playing dirty, June," I scolded her. "You know Andy can't say no to you."

She gave me a smug look and smiled wide. "Can't I come, Andy?"

"You're fifteen. This is so childish. You don't see Griffin bothering us to take him to Calishake."

"That's because Griffin is perfectly content playing his stupid video games. He doesn't voluntarily leave the house for anything!" she retaliated. "Come on, Andy. I'm the one that made you that bracelet."

I looked back at Andy, and, sure enough, he was being won over by her. I wished he'd have more of a backbone when it came to my siblings. It was sweet. But really?

"She has a point," he said to me with a shrug.

"Fine!" I groaned. "But you're sitting in the backseat, and you're only getting one scoop, not that five scoop sundae you always pull with Dad."

. . .

It was incredible how everyone in the community always got involved in the themes. When we walked in, Calishake was filled with people who came to dress up in their cute pastel clothes and enjoy the wholesome fun.

"This is legit," Andy said when he saw it. "It's like this every month?"

"Yep," I confirmed. "March is cottagecore, July is roller skates. Just...everyone wears roller skates. That's the theme," I laughed. "October is grunge. November is 50's style. Ooh, maybe next year you can come in May because it's space-themed."

"Every year, it's the same themes?"

"More or less," I said.

"With slight variations," June added. "Two years ago, the space month was vintage space, so there were a lot of old science fiction costumes and things like that. But this year, it was neon space, so the parlor was lit up by everything glow-in-the-dark. They painted the jukebox and the booths in fluorescent paint, and there were glow-in-the-dark stars everywhere. People came in with glow sticks all over them. It was awesome. I wish you could have come."

It made me miss coming here every month. I didn't know about the neon space theme in May.

We stood in the line to pick our ice cream, and Andy still hadn't decided on a flavor by the time we had to order. June and I went ahead of him. I chose black cherry cheesecake with extra cherries. June picked strawberry, just like she always did.

I glanced over, and Andy was still debating. The people in line behind him were impatient.

"Hey, babe, let's move it along," I coaxed.

"I can't decide..." he trailed off. "Should I get peppermint or peanut butter cup or banana cream?"

I gave him a minute, but I ordered banana cream pie with extra vanilla wafers after he still didn't pick. The line behind us clapped when we finally moved up to the cash register.

"Banana cream pie is delicious, don't worry," I assured him. Andy paid for us, and we went to a booth by the window to eat.

"You're right. This is really good," Andy said with a full mouth.

June laughed.

Andy got a phone call and, with trepidation in his eyes, showed me the screen. It was Carlotta.

"I don't want to answer," he murmured.

"Just answer. She'll keep calling," I told him.

He nodded and answered his phone. I stole a wafer while he spoke with Carlotta.

"What? Since when have we ever had a meal together?" he asked incredulously.

He held the phone away from him and mouthed, "Brunches twice a week."

Ugh. What was it about brunch that that woman found so appealing?

Going back to the conversation with his mom, Andy listened, trying to interrupt. He was unsuccessful in doing so. Finally, he said, "Yeah, here you go."

And he handed the phone to me.

No, no! Carlotta didn't like me even when she was in a good mood, let alone when she was irate. I refused to take the phone, but Andy kept prompting me until I finally answered.

"Hi, Carlotta," I said, with as kind a voice as I could muster.

"Apparently, my son loves you, and although I told him your relationship is futile, he won't listen to me. So, you'll be coming over twice a week for brunch with him. I don't want to hear your begrudging comments, and there's no storming out this time. For either of you. You or Andy break our terms, and I'm cutting him off."

She would cut him off? Over brunch?

It was her money that was paying for his college tuition. He'd do anything to keep that money around.

"Do you understand?"

"Yeah," I said.

I thought she would hang up, but then she added, "And don't you dare show up wearing those hideous shoes."

She didn't need to elaborate for me to know which shoes she was talking about- the black boots I wore when I first met her.

"Wear something classy, like a sandal or a heel. That would be nice."

"Hmm-hmm," I said, trying to keep myself from laughing.

She hung up.

I handed Andy his phone back and chuckled as I told him what she said. Before we knew it, we were all hysterically laughing.

Brunch with Carlotta was no laughing matter, but somehow Calishake could improve any situation. I ate my ice cream, wishing I could freeze time at this exact moment so I'd be surrounded by the people I loved most in the world, smiles pasted on our faces while we ate dessert. We were living the dream.

mid-morning scheming
July 2

We were at brunch- Carlotta's favorite part of the day- when the doorbell rang.

"I'll get it!" Carlotta squealed, raising herself from the chair and carefully placing her napkin on the table. She left the dining room to answer the door.

"Who's that?" I asked Andy.

He took a big bite of his jam toast. "No idea," he said with his mouth full. I laughed.

Andy always found a way to make mandatory brunches with his mother fun. Whether it was him being silly or making pop culture references that went over his mom's head, there was always something unexpected and fun about brunch.

As much as I complained in the morning when I had to get ready for Carlotta's meal, I enjoyed being Andy's ally when I was there. Like, she'd say something shady, and he'd stand up for me, willing to start an argument with her on my behalf. Or she'd act rude, and he'd tell an inside joke only me and him knew about.

It made me feel closer to Andy. We were on a team now, a team that went deeper than family ties. It was him and me until the end of the line.

I used my fork to push around my hashbrowns, shaping them into a face. Eyes and a wonky smile looked up at me. I elbowed Andy, and he snorted when he saw it.

Carlotta came back into the room and gave me a dirty look. "Don't play with your food, child. Didn't your parents ever tell you that?"

I believed people who made faces with their food grew up to be more creative and better people than those sticks in the mud who didn't. But I didn't tell Carlotta that.

"Andy, I have a surprise for you!" she said. There was an evil glimmer in her eyes, and I immediately felt uncomfortable. What did she have up her sleeve this time?

A girl I'd never seen came trailing in behind Carlotta.

She was stunning. She wore a boho skirt tied by the ankle and a draping tank top. A bandana was tied around her head.

Andy choked on his food.

He bent over, coughing, and I hit him on the back a few times. He recovered quickly and stood up, wiping his mouth and walking fast to greet the girl. Andy pulled her into a giant hug.

"Claire! Man, it's been so long!" he exclaimed, holding her shoulders as he backed up to get a good look at her.

"Tell me about it!" she agreed. She had a thousand-watt smile.

"Beck, this is Claire," Andy said, turning to me. "We were best friends growing up."

Claire. I flashed back to Andy's Human Studies project,

the night we spent talking endlessly. I remembered how he had mentioned his friend was recently diagnosed with cancer. He told me how hard it hit him.

"They were joined at the hip, these two," Carlotta said. "We all thought they'd end up marrying each other one day."

She glared right at me when she said this, making sure I got the point.

"I invited her to spend the rest of the summer here!" Carlotta smiled proudly.

"You're staying here?" Andy asked.

"Yeah. I was diagnosed a few months ago with cancer, and the hospital that I've been going to is so far from home. Carlotta's place is so much closer, and she offered for me to stay here until my treatments are finished," Claire said.

"I figured, what perfect timing!" Carlotta said. "Andy's home for the summer and I know how close you two are."

Carlotta hadn't done a single nice thing in her life. I knew this sudden visitor had everything to do with Carlotta realizing my and Andy's relationship was more serious than she believed. The epiphany swirled in her mind, haunting her.

As presumptuous as it was to think this childhood friend's arrival was all about me and not about her cancer...I was sure it was about me. Carlotta was trying to break us up.

I stood up to introduce myself.

"Nice to meet you! I'm Rebecca." There was an awkward pause where I held my hand out for her to shake, and she leaned in to hug me. But her hug won out; she wrapped her arms around me like she didn't even see my handshake attempt, which I was grateful for.

"How long have you two been together?" Claire asked.

"Almost a year," Andy said proudly. He wrapped his arm around my neck and planted a kiss on my temple.

"I never thought you'd date a girl this beautiful," she teased. "You spent all your free time reading comic books and playing with action figures. I didn't think you had it in you, Andy."

"Ha-ha." Andy rolled his eyes.

"Well, he still spends all his time reading comic books and playing with action figures, so I guess not much has changed," I laughed, and Claire looked relieved I joined in on the fun.

"Does he still have that Xeno Attack alien ship model thing?" Claire asked.

"I'm right here," Andy said since we weren't talking directly to him. But she didn't even glance his way.

"Yep. He brought it with us for the summer and got a new set to build next to it. They're on my dresser right now," I said.

"You're a real saint," Claire laughed.

"Hey!" Andy exclaimed, offended.

I wrapped my arms around him and smiled. "I like your Xeno Attack model ship," I assured him.

Carlotta gave the three of us a dark look. She hadn't expected us to get along.

"Let's sit down," she clapped her hands. We all followed

her back to the table. "Andy, I told her you'd take Claire to treatments. It's not like you have anything else to do, right?"

"Yeah, that's fine," Andy agreed.

Claire smiled and grabbed Andy's hand from across the table.

"Thanks, Andy."

I didn't like the way she looked at him.

the one who knew
July 9

"I don't like her," June said after we finished our movie.

It was supposed to be the four of us. Mom and Dad went out for a date night, so Andy said he'd help me keep my siblings entertained. But then Andy came with Claire, even though she wasn't invited.

"Yeah, well," I said, shrugging my shoulders.

We whispered while Andy and Claire were in the kitchen, getting more snacks for us.

"I like her," Griffin added. He wasn't as quiet as we were.

"Yeah, we *know*," I reminded him. He'd been telling Claire she was cute and pretty all night. He was using all his lines on her, even the ones he learned from movies. I warned him that if he repeated them, I'd wash his mouth out with soap.

"Just saying," Griffin muttered defensively. "She laughed

at all the right parts of the movie."

I narrowed my eyes. "Is that your only standard?"

"You don't laugh at the right times. You never laugh, even at the funny parts. And Andy laughs for too long after the jokes. It's weird."

I was wounded.

"What about me?" June asked seriously.

He looked her over with a thoughtful expression. "Nah, you're good."

June broke into a smile.

I rolled my eyes. "This is not the issue here."

"Yeah, the issue is that your boyfriend is in love with the super-hot childhood friend," Griffin laughed. I smacked his leg. "You're the one that let them go get snacks alone in the kitchen together."

"Griffin has a point," June said. "But it's not all Claire's fault. I mean, Andy's the one who brought her over here in the first place. I thought it would take longer for his loyalties to be swayed."

She wasn't wrong. It had been a week, and I could already feel myself getting phased out. I was his girlfriend, yet somehow, *I* was getting phased out.

"He's just taking her to treatments," I said, but it came out like a weak attempt at an excuse.

June looked at me with wide eyes. "And you don't see the issue in that? That's like, three hours of them hanging out together. *You* know. You used to take me to my treatments. We'd watch movies or read books or just talk. For hours. And it gets cold there, so he's probably letting her borrow his jacket and everything."

She was right.

"Fine. I'll go talk to Andy." I stood up and went into the kitchen.

Andy and Claire laughed as they tossed popcorn at each other, stray pieces of snacks littering the floor. I stood in the doorway, trying not to look as angry as I was. They were supposed to be getting snacks for all of us, not making a mess in my house.

They looked so natural together. Claire was tall and thin, supermodel style, so there wasn't a drastic height difference between them. Their chemistry from years spent together was undeniable.

They stopped when they saw me.

"Andy, can I talk to you alone?"

Claire excused herself from the room politely, which made me even angrier. She was too nice.

Andy came up to me and put his hands on my waist. "What's up, babe?"

I gave him a look, and he seemed genuinely confused, like he didn't understand what I was upset about. I would have thought he was faking, but as I looked into his eyes, I saw no malice in them. He was just that dumb.

"I get that Claire is your friend, and you're helping her, but my tolerance only goes so far," I said seriously.

"Is this about her coming to movie night?" he asked. He looked so innocent. "I was going to drop her off, but I know you hate when people are late, so I just brought her. I'm sorry, though. I should have checked in with you ahead of time. That's on me."

It was hard to be mad at him when he was apologizing. He made sense. It was a valid reason for bringing her. He knew I *hated* when people were late, so I couldn't very well be mad at him for that.

"You realize your mom brought her here to break us up, though, right?" I asked. He had to recognize that.

He nodded. "I know. But I can't just not spend time with her. She's my best friend."

I shook my head. "With the risk of sounding jealous-"

"You're jealous?" He looked at me, surprised. I was usually so confident in myself. At least, I pretended to be.

"Can you just listen? I'm saying this, fully aware of how it's going to sound, but a guy's girlfriend should be his best friend." Andy started to say something, but I kept talking. "I've seen it too many times where- like, in high school, I had this friend named Kacey. She was this guy's best friend. His name was Jake. Alright? So, Jake started dating this other girl, but his friendship with Kacey never changed. He spent just as much- if not more- time with Kacey than he did with his girlfriend, and everyone was getting on the girl because she confronted him about it. Everyone acted like she was the crazy one, but guess what?"

"What?"

"Jake broke it off with her because he'd made out with Kacey."

Andy smiled, and it annoyed me. I wasn't making a joke.

"I don't think I've ever heard you talk that much all at once."

It was usually Andy who went on the long-winded speeches.

"Yeah, well, it's important to me that you understand this." He was still smiling, and I pushed him gently. "I'm not kidding."

He pulled me close to him. "I'm not laughing," he said, even though he was. "I get it. But that was high school. We're in college now."

"It's the same principle," I mumbled against his sweater.

"Alright. I promise I won't call things off to be with Claire."

It wasn't just that, though. I was worried that he'd spend so much time with Claire that she would start taking over his heart. It would be gradual, and he wouldn't even realize it.

And I didn't want him to wake up one day and wonder what it would have been like if he'd dated Claire instead of me. I didn't want the uncertainties to pile up until he resented being with me. Those were the sort of things that people never planned to happen. I didn't want his current ignorance to be our future downfall.

But I didn't say anything. I didn't want to push Andy

away, so I just let the silence thicken between us. I hoped he understood how important it was to me. I hoped he learned from Jake and Kacey.

"Alright. I'm going to go take the popcorn for our second movie," he said, kissing my forehead.

I stuck around even after he left the kitchen. I had that sick feeling in my gut.

Mom always said I had good instincts- I got it from my grandmother on her side. Halmeoni was always so intuitive; even when I was little, she could see right through me. She knew my intentions before I even knew them. Halmeoni could tell you if a person was a good influence as soon as she met them, and she was never wrong.

Mom always said I had that trait too. "Your instinct never lies. Listen to it."

And my instinct was telling me that the Carlotta and Claire Scheme would be our downfall. I wished Halmeoni were here to confirm what I felt, but I didn't need her assurance. I knew I was right.

Claire appeared in the doorway as I analyzed what this new arrival meant for Andy and me.

"Hey, Becky," Claire said, calling me a nickname I'd never heard before. It sounded like an insult coming out of her mouth. "I just don't want you to feel uncomfortable about this whole thing. I know my being here is unexpected, and I just wanted to make sure there's no bad blood between us."

I smiled. "Of course not. We're all good."

"Good. Because I already told Andy how I feel about him, and he told me how much he loves you. Nothing is going on between the two of us."

She told Andy how she felt about him?

"What?" I asked. "When did you tell him that?"

"Today at treatment. I said I wanted to be with him, and he said he loves you." She looked unconcerned with everything she was saying.

I, on the other hand, looked like I was watching a horror film.

Andy knew Claire liked him, and he dared to act like I was overreacting a few minutes ago? When he knew all my fears were valid?

"He didn't even entertain the thought," she continued.

But he was letting Claire treat him like that. Andy was still having fun, throwing popcorn at her and taking care of her.

"You don't have to worry about him turning out to be Jake." She flashed a slight smile before turning and walking out of the kitchen.

She was listening to our conversation?

There were so many things I wanted to tell her. So many comebacks I had. But there was no point in getting into a fight with Claire when the real problem was Andy. It wasn't worth it, so I just stood there, dumbfounded, until Andy came to get me so they could start the movie.

I held up a finger. "You knew."

His face dropped.

I walked right past him and made them leave. There were no more movie marathons that night; I didn't want them in my house, sitting next to each other on the couch.

"But this is the best movie of the series!" Griffin complained.

"It's alright, little dude," Andy said, giving him a fist bump. "We can watch it some other time, and I'll bring over my signed copy of the comic for you to see, as long as you keep your grimy hands clean."

This seemed to settle things for Griffin, and he nodded eagerly.

June must have sensed Andy was in trouble because she didn't hug him when he started to leave. She just glared at him, taking my side loyally.

Andy tried to kiss me goodbye, but I turned my head.

He knew.

voicemails
July 11

I didn't answer Andy's calls for two days. Eventually, he resorted to leaving voicemails. At first, I didn't listen to them; I wasn't in the mood to hear his excuses.

He knew. It was as simple as that.

He acted like I was the irrational one.

After I told him all my concerns, he just verified my fears.

"*Nothing would ever happen between Claire and me,*" I mumbled, mimicking Andy. "*Don't worry, Beck. We're just friends. Ha-ha-ha.*"

I caved and listened to my voicemails after dinner.

I started with the first one he left.

"Rebecca, I know you don't want to listen to me, but it's not what you think. I told Claire it could never work with us and that I love *you*. Please just call me back."

And then the next one.

"I'm trying to give you space. I know you like that. But I wanted to talk with you and figure this out. It's nothing, and I need you to understand that. Call me."

Next one.

"I drove over to your house, but your mom said you were out. I don't know if you're actually out or if she's covering for you, but please talk to me. I'm going to wait outside your house for ten minutes, so if you're home and change your mind, come talk to me."

I wasn't home that time. I went out for boba with June, but Mom told me he had stopped by while we were gone.

I played the most recent voicemail.

"I don't know what to say." He sounded tired. "I've been thinking about it a lot and...I messed up. But I have to be there for her. She's going through a hard time, and we're best friends. It's that simple. I'm sorry if it makes you uncomfortable, and I realize I need to tone it back. But I'm not going to abandon her.

We only have a few weeks until we'll be back in Boston, and then you won't have to worry about her. But while I'm here...while *she's* here, things are different. And-"

The voicemail cut off.

I double-checked if there was another message, but there wasn't. I started to worry. Andy would have left another message to finish what he was saying. Andy didn't let anyone cut him off.

He once left six voicemails, all picking up where he got cut off last time. And that was about a stupid *book*. Let alone something actually important.

I looked at the time stamp on the voicemail. 3:32. It was three hours ago.

It was probably nothing. I tried to shake the feeling that something terrible had happened.

But maybe he got in a crash while he was leaving the message. Maybe he was in the hospital or in a coma.

Usually, I wasn't so unreasonable. But everything was flipped upside down, and I couldn't be sure of anything.

I called Mr. Bynes, but he didn't answer.

I was overreacting. Nothing bad happened to Andy.

But the thought freaked me out so much that I got in my car and drove to Mr. Bynes' house, where Andy was staying.

When I got there, the door was ajar.

Oh my god, what if a burglar came in?

I crept in, trying to be as quiet as possible. I put my keys between my knuckles, ready to attack if anyone jumped out of the shadows.

"Hello?" I whispered. "Andy? Mr. Bynes?"

There was no answer, so I crept upstairs, my heart pounding in my chest. A creak came from Andy's room, and I swallowed my fear as I headed in. I walked slowly, keeping in mind all the ways to escape if I had to make a quick getaway.

I made it through the doorway, fully standing in Andy's room.

And that was when a hand grabbed me from behind the door.

I screamed my head off, slashing the air with my keys until I realized it was Andy's touch.

"It's just me," he said. "I didn't know how else to get you over here. You wouldn't talk to me."

He planned all of this?

"What is wrong with you!" I exclaimed, punching his arm. My heart was still racing. "I hate you!"

"Yeah, I kind of got that when you didn't return any of my calls." He moved away from the door and sat down on his bed.

"You're psychotic."

"Isn't it sweet that I know you so well I knew you'd come if I didn't finish my message? That's sweet, right? Come on." He smiled and held his arms out like he wanted a prize.

"Just a tip: next time, don't scare me half to death when I'm already mad at you," I said, still not smiling. "I'm here now. What do you want to tell me?"

He looked hurt that I wasn't more lighthearted.

"You're right. I should have told you about what Claire said. I'm torn because it's like I have to choose between my girlfriend or my best friend, and I'm just having a hard time."

I shook my head. He wasn't getting it right. "I'm not making you choose. I get that you have history with her. I get that she's your friend. But I'm not going to stand here while you two flirt right in front of me and pretend it's not flirting. I'm not going to stand here and be phased out of a relationship with you. I won't do it."

"Phased out?" he said, standing up. "I could never phase you out, Roo. I love you." He paused. "I'll figure it out, okay, but you're not going to get phased out. I'm just asking you to stick with me right now. For a few more weeks."

A few more weeks. A lot could happen in a few weeks.

"You trust me?" he asked.

Of course, I did. But all the time he spent with her was time spent away from me. And distance made it easier to compromise. It was easier to get detached when you weren't together.

And in that time apart, in those weeks before school started back up, what would become of us?

"I trust you."

I didn't tell him about my fear while walking through the house, searching for him. I didn't tell him that I was scared to death I'd find him making out with Claire.

the wise mr. bynes
July 30

Andy's dad always liked me, and since Carlotta hated me, he balanced the scale. I was sitting there at the dinner table with him. Andy was late, for the first time in his life. So, it was just Mr. Bynes and me.

I thought it would be awkward at first. But really, it wasn't. He reminded me of my grandpa, even though my grandpa died when I was young. Mr. Bynes was how I liked to picture my grandpa being.

"The summer always has a way of changing things, doesn't it?" Mr. Bynes said, adjusting his glasses. "How are you faring?"

I paused, debating whether or not to enlighten him about my troubles with his son.

"It's been difficult lately," I answered. "Andy's never been late before."

Mr. Bynes sighed, and I couldn't help but think of how much he reminded me of a teddy bear. He always wore a brown coat, and his eyebrows were permanently raised towards the middle like he was sympathetic to everything. He sounded like a cartoon character when he sighed.

"He and Claire were always very close," he said. "And now, after the diagnosis...he feels like he needs to be there for her. To save her. Try not to be so hard on him. I'm sure there will be a time when you need him to stick around just as much as he needs you right now."

I wondered if that was true. If there would be a time when I'd be glad I stayed through this rocky patch. If there would be a time I needed Andy so badly that the tables would turn, and he'd be the one putting up with my problems.

"Do you ever wish you had resolved things with Carlotta?" I asked. He took a moment of silence, and I felt bad I said anything. Maybe it wasn't appropriate. Maybe it was painful for him to talk about.

But then he answered without a trace of pain in his voice.

"No. I wish we had ended things sooner. It would have given me more time to get on with my life."

Mr. Bynes spoke so darkly.

There was a flicker in his eyes, and he tried to correct his sentence, realizing his statement probably wasn't the most comforting to someone who was wondering if she should break things off.

"But Carlotta has always been mean. I don't think we ever really loved each other. Maybe we did. But we married more out of fear than anything else."

"Fear?" I asked. "Of what?"

"Of our families' disapproval of us marrying someone else. Of being alone for the rest of our lives. Promise me you won't do that, Rebecca. Don't marry someone because you're afraid not to marry them. That's no way to live."

I wondered if he made Andy promise that as well.

I couldn't imagine Andy sitting down with his father when he was young, promising that he'd never marry a girl for the wrong reasons. Andy would have thought it was silly to talk about some future wife when he wasn't dating anyone.

But maybe Mr. Bynes never brought that up with his son after all. And that thought made the vow even more sacred. Like a secret warning whispered in the night.

"I promise," I said, but my throat was tight.

He checked his watch. "My son was supposed to be here thirty minutes ago."

Why did he have to remind me?

"Claire's having her treatment today. He went with her. He probably took her to get food before he dropped her off."

That was their system.

Mr. Bynes sighed. It wasn't in approval or disagreement; it was just there.

"No use in letting this food go to waste. It's a new recipe I tried."

Mr. Bynes had been cooking a lot since the divorce. Carlotta always had maids and chefs to do their work, so Mr. Bynes never had to cook before.

Living on his own, he discovered he loved cooking. When I first arrived for dinner tonight, he showed me the recipe cards he had printed out.

Tonight's meal was a rosemary chicken recipe he found on a food blog.

Before the divorce, he never even knew what a food blog

was.

But now, he was thriving, enjoying a new life where he cooked for himself.

I wondered how long it took to get to the point of thriving after a relationship.

"Let's eat before it gets cold," Mr. Bynes said.

It was already cold, but I didn't want to mention that. We started eating, and we sat in silence.

It was only a few minutes more until Andy came through the door with an urgent look on his face.

"The treatment took a little longer than it was supposed to," he said, coming around the table towards me. "Hi, babe." He kissed me on the cheek.

"Come eat. I'm trying out a new recipe," Mr. Bynes beamed with pride.

"I grabbed some food on the way home," Andy said. But then he glanced over at his dad and realized how rude that was. "But I'm still starving. You know me."

I was starting to think I didn't know him as well as I thought.

We didn't talk very much for the rest of dinner.

last chances
August 9

It had been a week since I last saw Andy. He texted me a few times, but other than that, we hadn't talked in a while. He said he was busy with family, but that really meant he was busy with her.

I called him.

We had things we needed to talk about, and as much as I didn't want to discuss it over the phone, I knew he wasn't home.

He answered. "Hey, Beck."

"Hey," I said, relieved that he picked up. "Can we hang out soon?"

I felt so desperate, asking for his attention like this.

"Yeah, sure." Andy sounded distracted.

"Are we still seeing the Xeno Attack movie in theaters?" I asked, smiling. "Remember when we made plans like, a year ago? It feels so long ago."

I think he was smiling on the other end. "Yeah, go ahead and get the tickets. I can pay you back. Hey, I'm kind of in the middle of something. Can I call you in a bit?"

My heart dropped. He didn't even have a few minutes to spare.

"How is she?" I asked.

Andy sighed.

"I understand she has this extenuating circumstance, but

I can't keep doing this," I said. "You can go. Call me back or don't. Whatever. But I'm getting tickets because that's what we said we were going to do when the movie came out. And I'm only getting two tickets, just for us. I'm not mad. I want you to be there, and we can spend the day together. Maybe get dinner after. Okay?"

"Hmm-hmm," he agreed half-heartedly. "Yeah, that sounds great."

"Bye."

"Okay. Talk to you later. Bye."

I threw my phone across the room. He'd better be there, or I'd kill him.

the cinema
August 14

I stood outside for twenty minutes underneath the lit-up marquee. Lots of people passed me while I was thinking about where Andy was.

I'd never gotten stood up before. Back in high school, when my friends weren't getting treated right by some guy, I always said they should dump him. Dump him because they had plenty of options anyway. I never thought I'd be the one standing out in the chill of the night, waiting for a boy who wasn't going to show up.

8:54. The movie started at 9:00.

Andy was never late, so I knew he wasn't coming at all. He wasn't even coming to watch Xeno Attack, his favorite book's adaptation.

I remembered when we first started hanging out, and he made me read the book. He said we'd see the movie together on opening night. It would be his gift. He'd get me a ticket and buy popcorn and the peanut butter candy I liked.

He promised.

We made all these plans.

If anything were going to save us, it would be the Xeno Attack movie.

But even then, he was still choosing her.

I rechecked my watch- five more minutes.

"Well, *I'm* not missing the movie," I murmured under my breath as I headed into the theater.

I bought the popcorn and the peanut butter pieces myself, and I sat down right in the middle of the seats, surrounded by all the couples and the families that came here with someone.

Just as the lights dimmed, I looked over to see June walking down the aisle toward me. Behind her were Griffin and my parents saying, "Excuse me," as they stepped over everyone.

Mom and June sat on either side of me.

"He's a stupid boy," Mom whispered, even though I knew she was just trying to make me feel better. She corrected herself, sensing my doubt. "Okay, he's smart. But he's a dumb genius. Dumb with girls. Comes from lack of experience."

I laughed.

"He'll either come to his senses or spend his days regretting he didn't realize it sooner," she said. "Either way, it'll get better after this."

"I sort of hope it's the former," I said, leaning my head against her shoulder.

"Time will tell, Rebecca."

And the movie started.

the end of the line
August 21

I was braiding June's hair when Dad called out to me.

"One second!" I yelled. I was almost to the end of the braids; I just needed to tie them up. When I was wrapping the elastic bands around the ends, my bedroom door swung open, and there was Andy, standing there breathless like he'd fought his way to get here, even though I knew it was only my meek dad who had stood between us.

I felt June tense up when she saw him. It wasn't just me he had abandoned lately. He hadn't seen her in a while either.

"We're busy," June said coldly.

"Rebecca, I think we need to talk this out," he said, completely ignoring June.

174

The Scent of Closure

I pretended to work on June's braids.

"Rebecca, would you listen to me?"

"We're busy," June repeated.

Andy gave her an annoyed glance, which did not help smooth things over with my sister. She huffed and stood up, storming out of the room dramatically. June turned her body sideways as she slipped past him through the doorway as if brushing against him would be the worst thing in the world.

"I'm not in the mood-"

"Just listen to me," he interrupted. "I'm telling you it's nothing, okay? I'm standing here trying to tell you *nothing* is going on between us."

"Ha! That's hilarious," I fake laughed. "It's nothing? You're hanging out with some girl almost every night and choosing her over your girlfriend. That's not nothing, Andy!"

He sat down on the edge of my bed, and I shook my head.

"Get up," I said. And he did.

"She's having a hard time, and I need to be there for her. You don't get it, but she's my best friend."

Best friend. He was an idiot, and he knew it. The second he said it, there was a flash across his face like he wished he could take it back.

"She's your best friend." I smiled through my pain. "Is this the type of stuff your mom said to your dad when she was sleeping around with her so-called friends?"

It was a low blow, and I knew it.

"That's not fair."

"You know what's not fair? That I was stood up on a date last week because you were with her. It's not fair that I get two-word replies every time I text you because you're too busy texting her. That's not something I can deal with anymore. I *told* you that. And you said to trust you. Look at where that's gotten me."

He was trying to come up with a defense. I could see the gears turning in his head. He was always so good at figuring things out.

"She needed me," he said, exasperated.

"So did I."

Andy threw up his hands. "I don't know if this is what it's like for you...if you're just used to having all the attention, but not everything is about you, Rebecca."

He only called me Rebecca when he was upset.

"I mean," he continued, "you're the center of attention in your family unless June is in the hospital. You were the popular one in high school, the popular one in college. And I know I'm like, some peasant that you saved from the bottom of the social ladder when you started hanging out with me, so I'm sure this must be shocking, but I do have friends besides you. I have a life that doesn't revolve around you. You are not my everything. I know you think you are, but you're just one part of my life. One little part of my life. That's all."

Just a little part of his big life.

I bit my lip and looked away from him.

"Well, you're no part of mine," I said.

He came to my side and held my arm, clinging to me because he knew he messed up. I didn't push him away. I just sat there.

"Beck, you know that's not true. I just say things I don't mean."

I shook my head. "Get out."

"Beck," Andy said softly. He talked so sweetly. And I loved that he was back to calling me Beck.

I wanted to punch him.

"Get out," I repeated even more firmly.

He got up off his knees and started to leave. He turned around when he reached the doorway. "So, what do we do now?"

I groaned. "Nothing! We don't do anything. We're done."

There was a long stretch of silence where I played with the drawstrings on my sweatpants, and he just watched me. I didn't want to look up at him because I knew seeing his face would make me forgive him.

But he didn't deserve to be forgiven. Not yet.

"If we'll never see each other again, can you at least give me back my sweatshirt? And that model ship from Xeno Attack?"

He *had* to be kidding.

I didn't know if he was trying to be funny or if he was dead serious. He wanted all his stuff back. Right now, after he came over, clearly in the wrong, and gave some roundabout apology.

"Fine." I stood up and rummaged through my middle drawer, grabbing his tie-dye orchid sweatshirt he said I could have. I balled it up and threw it at him.

"You want your stupid action figure too?" I threw that.

What else did he leave in my room?

His comic book. I threw it at him.

He caught it, but it crumpled in half, and I found enjoyment in the destruction of his precious book. Andy just stood there, holding everything in his arms.

"Why are you still standing here?" I wished he would leave so I could scream or cry or break something. I really wanted to kill him, but I also didn't want him to see how much he'd gotten to me, how much I let his words mess with my mind. I didn't know what the balance between that was- between wanting to hurt someone and not letting them see how much they hurt you.

"My Xeno ship," Andy said.

I grabbed the stupid ship off my dresser and hurled it at his head as hard as I could. I didn't think it would actually hit him, but he doubled over, holding the side of his face.

That would leave a mark.

high school parallels
August 21

I remembered a party back when I was in high school. Most of the kids had gone home, and the rest of us started playing truth or dare.

Jake picked truth, and he was asked which of us girls was his favorite.

I thought I had a shot. I had my head down, sure, acting like I was humbled by the possibility of someone else getting chosen.

But I knew Jake's answer was going to be me. I didn't have any doubt in my mind because Jake was my best guy friend. He was a big part of my life. Honestly, I would have chosen him over half of my girl friends. He helped me out a lot, and we always had fun when we were together. I was just so sure he would say he liked me best.

"Kacey," he said, hardly even hesitating.

I remembered how hurt I was that day. I pretended to laugh it off, but I was hurt.

Because he meant so much to me, and I meant so little to him.

I realized it was a stupid, immature question. But it didn't make the pain any less real.

It had been four years since then, but there I was, back in the same boat.

Three months ago, I would have said I was Andy's favorite person. But he chose her over me and never even apologized for it.

How could I get over something like that?

PART 4: SOPHOMORE YEAR

sophomore slump
August 25

A few boys threw a frisbee across the campus, and I ducked as it almost whacked me in the head.

Summer was officially over. It was great to be back.

As long as I didn't have to see Andy, this year would be a piece of cake.

I was excited to learn more in my classes, and I looked forward to seeing Hillary again after our months apart.

Jamie from Ledger's Records was happy to keep me employed now that I was back in town, and I couldn't wait to get back to work. I missed that record shop so much while I was gone and knowing that it was waiting for me was the only thing that kept me going.

"Beck!" a voice called from behind me.

Ugh. I kept walking, pretending I didn't hear Andy, but after a few steps, I paused. He'd chase me down. He was a lot faster than me with those long legs of his, so there was no point in trying to outrun him.

I spun around with a deathly glare on my face.

Sure enough, there he was, jogging up to me, his backpack thudding against his lower back with each step.

"Beck, wait up," he panted when he reached me.

A dark bruise overtook the flesh on his eye where the Xeno Attack ship had hit him. I didn't *mean* to hit him, but it wasn't like I could tell that to his black eye.

"I think you've said enough," I spat, turning away from him. He was right behind me, though, not missing a beat.

"What I said...I didn't mean that. It came out wrong, okay? You know that's not what I meant," he argued.

"Do I know that?" He never apologized for it. He just left it out in the open. And now he expected me to forgive him, just like that? After everything that happened this summer? After he'd given me days to analyze every word of what he'd said?

"I don't know what you want from me. I apologized-"

"No, you didn't."

He looked genuinely confused, as if he thought he'd said sorry. Andy's dark eyes were full of regret; I noticed it even though I pretended not to.

"Well, I'm sorry. I'm really sorry about everything this summer. That wasn't fair to you. But I'd like to remind you that *I* wasn't the one who brought her," Andy specified.

I spun around again, jaw locked, anger burning in disbelief.

He always got away with technicalities. You could tell he

was that sort of kid. The whole, *"The rules said the last person to cross the finish line is the rotten egg, but I didn't even cross the finish line, so it's not me"* sort of thing.

"No, you just let her cling to you for three months. My mistake."

I kept walking. He tried to grab my arm and hold me in my place, but I wriggled out of his grasp. "Stop! Just go away!" I exclaimed.

I got a few feet away until he called out to me.

"So, you're going to let my mom win? Just like that? This is what she wants. She wants you to freak out and break up with me, so she never has to deal with you again. I never thought you'd play along with her schemes," he scoffed.

"No. *You* played along with her schemes," I corrected. "And I'm tired of you trying to act like you didn't."

He winced, knowing I was right.

"Just leave me alone," I said.

He let me walk off, and I thought, just maybe, he'd leave me alone for the year. I would have been fine with that.

. . .

I walked into my dorm room and immediately burst into a smile despite my argument with Andy.

"Hillary!" I exclaimed, rushing toward her.

She didn't like hugs, but this occasion required one. She wrapped her arms around me, tight.

"I put your name on the form!" Hillary said, smiling wide.

"I put your name too!" I squealed.

Hillary and I were roommates again, and nothing could make me happier.

I didn't know what I'd do without Hillary, and I was glad I wouldn't have to find out.

"How was your summer?" I asked.

"Horrible," Hillary rolled her eyes. "We toured with Felt all summer, and then people started liking our lead."

"Isn't that good?" I asked.

"*No*," she growled. "Because now we don't have a singer. He got signed to a label and sold us out. He didn't even try to get them to sign us as a band! He went solo and dropped us, just like that."

"Randy was an idiot anyway. I'm sure he'll be washed up, and no one will even remember him in a few years," I said, trying to be comforting.

"Yeah," Hillary said evilly, relishing the idea of getting revenge on Randy. "Anyway, how was your summer?"

I raised my eyebrows. "Well, Andy and I are done." Her jaw dropped. "Yeah, he was wrapped around this girl's finger. She was a 'family friend'. He spent all summer with her."

She scoffed. "It's surprising enough that Andy can get *one* girl to love him, let alone two."

Hillary teased, but she understood the appeal. She knew how sweet Andy could be, how kind and caring he was.

"I saw him like, thirty minutes ago. Why is he all beat up?" Hillary asked.

"He's not beat up!" I exclaimed defensively.

"Looked like it to me."

"Yeah, well, I accidentally hit him."

Hillary looked surprised. "Good for you. He probably deserved it anyway. Personally, I always thought you could do better than Andy. He's neurotic. I mean, yeah, he's adorkably cute and caring, he gives great gifts, and he worships you-"

"I don't think that's helping," I cut her off.

"Let's focus on the neurotic part," she said definitively.

the giver
September 1

I lay on my bed, headphones in, listening to my music with the volume as loud as possible. June always reminded me that loud music was bad for my hearing and that I'd probably be deaf by forty years old. But she wasn't here to scold me for it.

My eyes were closed, and I lay completely still, letting the song wash over me. Sometimes, I'd get so absorbed in the music that I forgot where I was. I called it a song coma- I was conscious of the music but nothing else. It felt good to trap myself in that reality, where I was living but didn't have to feel pain, a world where I could disconnect from everything and reside in the bliss of prose.

So, when a hand touched my arm, pulling me out of my song coma and into reality, I freaked.

I kicked my foot out and grabbed the person's arm instinctively. But as soon as my eyes opened and I registered what was going on, I settled down. It was just Hillary.

I took out my headphones.

"You know you're not supposed to interrupt me-"

"-When you're simping with your eyes closed, I know," Hillary finished. "But I think you're gonna want to be interrupted for this."

It was doubtful.

"What is it?" I asked. I was careful not to show the annoyance in my voice. Hillary was just trying to help.

"It's a surprise," she said with one eyebrow raised. I sat up more, and she handed me a blindfold. "Just put it on. It's part of the ambiance."

Ambiance. That was definitely a term Andy would have used. My heart fluttered a bit at the thought that he was the one behind all this.

I tried to stop myself from getting excited at the possibility, but I couldn't help it.

I'd spent the last week thinking a lot about everything that happened with Claire. And I'd been feeling a little sorry about how I handled things. Only a little. Mostly because I knew Andy wouldn't do anything with her. I recognized that so easily now.

Part of me wanted to apologize for not even trying to see his side of the matter. I wanted to text him and own up to my mistakes, hoping that he would own up to his.

But I was too prideful to take the first step at apologizing. Andy was the reason we weren't together.

I hoped this surprise would be him saying sorry.

The blindfold prevented me from seeing anything, so Hillary guided me through the dorm hallways. At first, I thought we were going to Andy's room, but we took a right instead of a left.

I didn't realize I had the route memorized, but I did. Even without being able to see, I knew my way to him. That had to count for something, right?

"Can't you give me a hint?" I asked when Hillary and I had been walking for a long time.

"No, I can't."

I wanted to ask if Andy made her promise not to give me any details, no matter how much I asked. I liked to think he did.

We walked for a while longer before we stopped. Hillary knocked on a door, and I heard it creak open a moment later. Silence surrounded us as we stepped inside the room.

"He's the best with gifts," she whispered before she left.

It *was* Andy!

I had to remind myself not to act too eager with whatever he surprised me with. I wanted him to work for it. He needed to sweat it for a while.

While I was planning out how I'd react to whatever was

about to happen, I felt someone approach me from behind. The knots on my blindfold were getting untied.

I knew it was Andy. I knew it from the way he breathed and how he felt when he was next to me.

The blindfold came off, and I was standing in a room entirely illuminated with stars covering the walls and ceiling. They were glow-in-the-dark stars on steroids. They were blue and bright, and dozens floated in midair around me.

I knew there must be a string attaching them to the ceiling, but it looked so pretty I didn't want to ruin the magic with logic.

I spun in a slow circle, holding out a hand as I gazed at the beauty of the makeshift galaxy. And when I turned around, I saw Andy standing there, hands in his pockets. He was wearing that striped sweater he looked so good in.

He was making it difficult to play hard to get, and he hadn't even opened his mouth yet. Andy had always been good with sweet talk. He won me over every time.

"Beck, I'm so sorry about everything that happened this summer," he said, taking my hands in his. "It was supposed to be these great few months, and then Claire came back, and everything got turned upside down. And that's on me. You didn't deserve that, and I feel awful."

I didn't say anything, but I was already forgiving him.

"Her treatments are ending this week, and then she'll head back home. We're hoping the worst of it is over."

I was happy for her; I was. I didn't wish sickness on

anyone. Especially not after seeing cancer rob my June Bug of so much. But judging from the look on my face, he realized this wasn't the best time to be bringing Claire up again.

He started talking fast to bypass that.

"But that's not what this is about. I'm sorry, Beck." He smiled. "I'm not good at the whole apology thing. But I'm trying."

He was doing so good, but I didn't want to tell him that. Other than the little Claire hiccup, it was perfect so far.

"More than anything, I really hate what I said the night we fought. It was mean, and I want you to know that you're not just some little part of my life. You are my everything. My whole world and galaxy."

We're standing in a galaxy, I wanted to squeal. But I just hid a smile as he wrapped his arms around me.

"You're the best thing that has ever happened to me," he said.

I broke my silent streak and whispered against his neck, "You're my everything too."

This was why I loved Andy so much. He always went to such great lengths to prove how much he loved me. There was no doubt in my mind that I was his girl, and it was hard to remember why I ever doubted his loyalty this summer.

Andy reached in his pocket and pulled out something small. He put it in my hand, and I squinted to inspect it in the dim lighting.

It was a silver guitar pick on a necklace with a personalized message that read: *You're my galaxy.*

I traced the words with my finger, feeling more connected to him now than I ever did before. He'd done something special, given me a gift so meaningful that I could hold it forever. I could wear it around my neck and know, without any doubt, that he was mine and I was his.

It was nice having a boy be mine.

Andy took the necklace and brushed my hair over my shoulder. He put the chain around my neck, fastening the clasp in the back. And then he kissed my jawline.

"I'm sorry," he said, in between kisses.

"You really know how to give a grand apology," I teased, smiling against his touch.

We stood there, swaying and dancing in the middle of a dorm room galaxy, an entire universe to call our own.

auditions are exhausting
September 23

I had protested when Hillary first gave me a newsboy cap to wear but, now that it was on, I was sort of vibing with it.

"This is the dumbest thing I've ever worn in my life," Andy said from behind me.

I turned to see what ridiculous outfit Hillary had him in, and I burst out laughing. He wore a red tracksuit and a gold chain. Oversized sunglasses covered his eyes.

He dropped his head in a mix of disappointment and irritation, moving his sunglasses down to the bridge of his nose so I could see his eyes.

"That's perfect!" Hillary exclaimed, clapping her hands.

Andy was exasperated. "What about *this*..." he said, gesturing to his costume, "...is perfect?"

"How many times do I have to tell you guys this? You have to *look* like a music producer if you want the auditions to be taken seriously."

We looked at her dubiously.

"What about you? You get to wear normal clothes," I pointed out.

"That's because I'm in the band. The band's image needs to be authentic." She acted like she was talking to children. "Come on. We don't want to be late. Let's go find us a lead singer!" Hillary whooped as she strutted out of the dorm room.

"She's insane," Andy complained.

"I kind of like the fit," I said. "It's growing on me."

He raised his eyebrows in amusement. "Yeah?" he asked, walking toward me.

"No, don't!" I exclaimed, laughing as he grabbed me around the waist. We laughed as we followed Hillary down the hallway. We'd gotten so close since our reconciliation. I think this was the closest we'd ever been. We weren't taking ourselves too seriously, and we were actually having *fun*.

I thought this year was going to be the best.

. . .

We sat in the theater for three hours, listening to tone-deaf people audition for Palm Trees and Power Lines. I was half asleep, resting my head on Andy's shoulder. I think he was grateful for the sunglasses so he could sleep without anyone seeing.

Hillary stood up from her drum seat and clapped her hands, getting everyone's attention.

"Before one more person auditions, I want to remind you that our band has toured with Felt! Okay? Our last singer got signed to a label! So, I'm gonna need you guys to step it up because I'm not impressed by anything we've seen. So. Step. It. Up." She clapped with every word.

The auditionees gave her dirty looks, but she shrugged.

"Next!" I called out, and Andy jumped at the sound of my voice.

"Quieter, please. I was having a good dream," he groaned. "Why is this taking so long? I'm blaming you."

My mouth dropped open. "Me? Blame Hillary!"

"*You're* the one who did all the ads. You told everyone you know about it, and let's be real, you know more people than both me and Hillary combined. It's your fault we're only halfway through the list. Next time, narrow it down to only the people you know by name, not everyone who nods your way when they pass you in the hall."

I stuck out my tongue.

I checked the clipboard for names as the new singer came on the stage. The girl wore her hair in two rows of buns reaching her waist.

"Let's change up the song," Hillary called out, looking bored. "If I have to hear this song one more time, I will die. Let's do Pavements by Red Light. You know that song, Grunge?"

The girl glanced back and smiled at the nickname. "Hit it."

I nuzzled back up to Andy, ready to fall back asleep. But then the girl started singing with this raw, beautifully tortured voice, and I sat up instead. So did Andy, and Andy didn't even have a good ear.

Not only was she an incredible singer, but she was a good performer, jumping around the stage and dancing in a quirky way that only she could pull off.

I checked the roster to see what her name was. Gale Brown.

By the second chorus, I'd already circled and underlined her name, knowing there was no one else who could compete with her.

Sure enough, Hillary gave Gale a standing ovation and a round of applause as soon as the song was finished. "That!" she yelled. "That is exactly what we're looking for. Are we all in agreement?"

We all nodded.

And just like that, Palm Trees and Powerlines had their

new lead.

candles
October 8

"Give me two scents you like," June said as soon as I answered the phone. She didn't even say hello.

"It's one in the morning here, remember?"

Andy's new roommate, Paul, had a party that night, and I had only gotten back a few minutes before June called. It was a good thing I wasn't sleeping, or I'd be mad she interrupted my beauty rest. The last time June woke me up for no reason, I hid all my clothes for a week so she couldn't borrow them. It turned out to be a bigger inconvenience for me than for her, but June was still pretty upset that she didn't get to wear my summer dress.

"Rebecca, what's your favorite? Like, if you were going to order two candles right now, what kinds would you get?" June asked impatiently.

"Are you getting me a gift? Because I'd rather have perfume-"

"No, it's not a gift for you!" she groaned. "I'm starting my own candle-making company. I put up a poll the other day, and 89% of my followers said they'd buy candles if I started selling them, so I'm trying to figure out what scents to make. I would already have a list if you'd answer my question instead of being obnoxious."

She was making her own candle company? At sixteen! I didn't have a sister; I had an entrepreneur!

"I don't know. Like lavender and butterscotch?"

"Okay, good. Thank you," June said.

She paused, and I resisted the urge to groan. Whenever she paused like that, she wanted something. She was great at getting her way. She acted all sweet and innocent and then asked for a huge favor. At least I could tell when it was coming.

"What do you want?" I asked skeptically.

"Nothing. I found a dress when I went thrifting, and I'm sending it your way soon. And there's a little koi pond teacup so that when you fill it up, it looks like a koi is swimming at the bottom."

It threw me off when she didn't ask for something right away. I dropped my guard and said, "Aww, thank you!"

"I need an investor," she blurted out.

"What?" I exclaimed.

She was a snake, slithering her way into my pocket and stealing all my cash while I was off daydreaming about a little koi teacup.

"Mom and Dad bought me a candle-making kit, but they said I have to pay for the rest myself. And the kit comes with tin jars, but they're ugly. Rebecca, I can't have ugly candle jars if I want to make a business for myself! It's all about creating an image. My image needs to be chic, like the ones they sell at the trendy stores."

I sighed.

"You're going to stick with it?" I asked. She did this a lot, getting into new phases and growing tired of them fast. "I'm not giving you money if you're going to quit in a week."

"Me? Never," June said.

That didn't exactly instill confidence, but it was as good as I'd get.

"I'll pay you back once I get up on my feet," she assured me. And for some reason, I believed her.

"Fine," I agreed. "I'll send you the money tonight, but I want a lavender candle."

"Deal."

the third song after pavements
November 4

"Radio station contests are a hoax," Andy said.

"You know, I love your constant skepticism and can't-do attitude, but that's not the vibes we need in this room right now. Okay?" I faked a smile.

Andy didn't understand because he'd never been into music. He wasn't the one who had spent hours in his room with four devices spread out on the bed, ready to call the radio station at the drop of a hat.

That was me. And I'd won before.

Me, Andy, Paul, and Hillary sat cross-legged on the floor of my dorm, in a little circle with our phones and a radio in the middle of us.

"Paul, what about the phone you have from your internship at Marx Point?" I asked.

Paul wore beanies, grew his hair out long, and painted his fingernails black. He was practically the poster boy for Marx Point, the tech company.

"The phone is only for work. No personal usage," Paul answered.

"What's more important? Work or the last concert of Red Light?" I reminded him. I wouldn't say he was as big of a Red Light fan as me, but he was pretty close.

"Fine. But if they track the usage on this phone, which they will because it's Marx Point, and I get fired, I'm gonna kill you." He pulled out the phone anyway.

"Okay, so we have five phones," I said.

"Seven," added Hillary, pulling two phones from her backpack pocket.

"Where'd you get *two* other phones? Did you rob someone?" Andy asked. He was kidding, but really, he wasn't.

Hillary raised an eyebrow mysteriously while she smirked. "Nobody needs to know."

The song on the radio ended, and the host started talking.

"This is D-Jaycee coming at you from KWAZ. We have four tickets for Red Light's Farewell Tour coming up. To win, all you have to do is call at the start of the third song after Pavement,

Red Light's greatest hit. If you're the 29th caller, you've won!"

Third song after Pavement.

The music started playing back up, and we sat in silence, waiting for the key song to begin.

We all had the KWAZ contact in our- and in Hillary's case, some randos'- phones, and our fingers were anxious to dial.

Andy looked dubious while staring at his phone.

"Good vibes," I reminded him. "Good vibes."

And then the third song after Pavement started. Time to shine, folks.

We all dialed in. This wasn't about speed; it was about timing, so we scattered our calls by seconds. The 29th caller was the goal.

"Busy," Paul said. He was trying again on the other phone.

"Busy," I announced.

"Busy." Hillary.

"Busy." Andy.

"Busy. Busy." Hillary again.

We all redialed.

My heart was pounding so hard. Red Light tickets sold out minutes after they went on sale, and I'd been trying to figure out a way to sneak into the concert when they came to Boston. Paul was in the same boat. We were both dying to see them one last time for their farewell tour. This was our one chance.

"It's ringing!" Andy exclaimed.

I leaned over toward him, trying to listen to what was

happening on the phone.

"Keep calling, Rebecca!" Paul reminded me. I dialed again.

Andy shouted.

"What, what!" I exclaimed, almost dropping my phone.

Andy put it on speaker so we could hear.

"-the 29th caller! What's your name?"

He had to yell "Andy" over the three of us, who were cheering and yelling as loud as we could. We abandoned the phones in our hands and jumped up and down together. We won tickets to Red Light!

Andy looked up at him, laughing, tongue in cheek, shocked that he, of all people, had just won a radio contest.

"A hoax, huh?" I smirked.

. . .

"So, are there going to be like, mosh pits?" Andy asked.

Palm Trees and Powerlines was his first concert, and we'd spent most of it dancing in the parking lot outside. He didn't know what to expect at the Red Light show.

"Probably," I answered. "But that's okay. We can dip out whenever you want." I knew he didn't like crowds, so I was perfectly content with stepping to the back if it meant I could take my boyfriend to see my favorite band.

"Okay, so we can back out of the mosh pits," he said. I nodded in confirmation. "What else do I have to know?"

"Bro, you'll be fine," Paul dismissed. "Just go with it."

But I knew Andy didn't just "go with" anything. He spazzed out about any plans we made, and he overthought every detail until he talked himself out of everything. This concert was no small feat for him.

"We're all going to be right there with you," I assured him. "We'll get a drink and buy some tour merch before we go in because the lines get too long if we wait until after. We'll get a nice, comfortable spot where we can all stand together. It'll be chill, Andy. If you feel uncomfortable at any point, we'll step into the hallways. Okay?"

That seemed to put him at ease.

"You still want to go?" I asked. I didn't want to force him to do anything he didn't want to.

He smiled. "Are you kidding? I'm psyched. Freaked out a little? Sure. But that's only because my parents were unhinged and never listened to music when I was growing up, so therefore, *I* never really listened to music. And in high school, I didn't have friends that went to concerts. I had friends that built action figure sets on the weekends. So, I'm just a late bloomer."

A very late bloomer.

But I didn't say it because I didn't want him to feel bad. Hillary didn't usually monitor her words, though, so she joked, "An *extremely* late bloomer."

"Better than being the dorky nine-year-old at the concert that all the teenagers think is weird," Andy retaliated.

Hurt flashed across Hillary's face. "*Hey!*" she exclaimed,

reaching over to smack him upside the head. "I told you guys that in confidence! That was a rough time for me," she pouts.

We went back to scrolling through our phones, searching for outfits for the concert. Andy had no sense of style, so we prepared his outfit for him. It might have seemed juvenile to plan our outfits so we'd look like an effortlessly synced, cool group of friends, but you had to go out and get that main character life.

Hillary and I had matching Red Light shirts we were going to wear. She'd wear hers with fishnets, a short skirt, and a leather jacket. I'd wear mine with a turtleneck and a pair of plaid pants.

Paul would wear black jeans, a Red Light sweatshirt, and a burnt orange corduroy jacket.

"I don't have a Red Light shirt," Andy pouted. Andy never cared about the latest trends, and he thought style was overrated. But the punk band shirt was sending him over the edge.

"I got you, babe," I said. After a quick search on my phone, I pulled up a Red Light ugly sweater picture. "This. This is what you'll be wearing."

He pushed the phone away and rolled his eyes, but when I showed it to the rest of the group, they laughed and agreed: *That* had Andy written all over it.

"I'm going to look like a dad who got stuck supervising his kids at a concert," Andy protests.

"More like a grandpa," Hillary cackled.

"Don't worry, man," Paul joined in, slapping Andy's

shoulder. "I'll let you borrow a jacket, and you'll be as cool as a cucumber."

We all burst out laughing.

"I'm going to find three other people to take to the concert if you keep teasing me like this," Andy said, trying to hide a smile.

We all pretended it was a real fear of ours, pleading with him until he gave in just to make us shut up.

"I'm ordering the sweater," I confirmed. "We're all going to look *amazing*. Even you, Grandpa."

the study room
November 13

Andy spent an insane amount of time in the study rooms. He said it helped him think. Each of the rooms had one glass wall, and it overlooked the campus. Most of the trees had already lost their leaves, so it wasn't as pretty as last month, but it was still somewhat serene to be five stories up, looking out over the world.

He was the one who made me like the rooms; I always thought they were confining before.

I knocked on the door before I went in. Andy asked me to meet him there.

He was sitting on the bench, all his school possessions spread out beside him: his laptop, notebook, and textbooks.

And he had that look on his face. The look he got when he had a new plan.

"Cambridge has spots open for students that want to study abroad. I just applied," he said. He seemed almost worried, waiting for my reaction.

"That's amazing!" I exclaimed, walking toward him.

"I don't know how we're going to figure this out. I kind of thought you'd freak out, but you're not the one freaking out. It's me freaking out."

"Andy," I said, putting a hand to his face. I always had to snap him out of it when he got into his babbling trances.

He stopped talking, looking at me with his innocent, childlike brown eyes.

"This is Rebecca Dae and Andy Bynes we're talking about," I said. "Nothing is going to split us apart."

For the most part, I believed what I was saying.

"And I'm *so* proud of you. How many people can say their boyfriend is going to be an actual aerospace engineer?"

"Well, technically there's a lot-"

"That was rhetorical." I realized he wasn't the only space genius in the world. But he was *my* only space genius.

We both smiled and kissed.

"I probably won't even get in. It's a tough program," he said.

We both knew he'd get in. He'd be at Cambridge before August ever came.

dan and the concert
November 30

I stopped at the gas station on the way home from Hazy's, where I visited Andy during his shift.

It was mid-afternoon, and the sun was so bright that it warmed my hands on the steering wheel even though it was almost winter.

The Red Light concert was tonight. I still had a few hours to get ready before we needed to head over to the venue. We had floor tickets, so we'd need to get there early if we wanted to get close by the stage.

I got distracted, thinking about the upcoming concert, and almost forgot to pull the nozzle out of my gas tank.

I paid and waited for my receipt, but it never came.

I rolled my eyes. I needed to stop coming to this gas station. They always made me go inside to ask for a receipt. Next time, I'd remember to go to the gas station by the campus. I wouldn't come here again.

A little bell chimed above my head as I stepped inside.

Almost immediately, I knew something was wrong.

The man behind the counter stood stiffly, watching me with wide, knowing eyes, trying to tell me something.

And then, in the mirror above the register, I saw a guy ducked down behind the counter, holding a gun to the cashier's body.

And he looked right at me in the reflection.

I tried to back up and make an escape, but the criminal popped up and aimed the gun at me.

He was screaming orders at me, but I couldn't hear. I could only hear the sound of blood rushing through me, the sound of my heartbeat pulsing through my veins.

I couldn't think of anything except that I would get shot right then, and I wouldn't make it to the concert. And even if he didn't shoot me, I'd have to give a statement to the police, and I'd still miss the show.

"Get down!" the man shouted, coming around the corner to put the gun against my head.

I dropped to my knees. He grabbed my arms and placed them above my head. I didn't fight back; I just did what he said.

I didn't know if that made me brave or a coward.

Last week, Hillary and I watched a movie about a bank robbery, and all the people just lay on the floor, terrified. Nobody tried to stop the robber, and I thought that was the dumbest thing in the world. They could have stopped him if they tried.

But now that I was living it, I knew there was no other choice.

I was going to die there. I just knew it.

"I'll give you the money," the cashier said.

He started to open the register, but the thief aimed the gun at him again, making him put his hands up in the air.

What would happen if he shot me? Would I immediately

die, or would I live a while longer, dying slowly on the dirty ground of a gas station, next to the stand of peanuts?

The burglar walked to the cash register and ordered the cashier to hand over the money.

"Don't think about pressing any call button."

I looked up at the two of them. Money was being exchanged. The criminal was getting what he wanted.

He turned around, faced me, and took a step forward.

Would he leave? Maybe that would be it. I'd be a little shaken up, I'd call Andy to talk me through it, and then I'd go home. Maybe we could even make the concert.

But then the cashier got a sudden burst of energy, and he tried to overpower the robber while his back was turned.

I put my head to the floor and pressed my hands against my ears. I didn't want to hear what was happening.

But the gunshots rang loud and clear no matter what I tried.

And I just stayed there, frozen in place, even after the body fell to the ground and the criminal ran off.

I just laid there, hyperventilating.

People always said that adrenaline gave people extraordinary abilities, like how moms can move a burning car to save their kids.

But there was no strength gained from my shaking hands.

I didn't stand up and go after the guy. I didn't call the police. I didn't help the cashier who was dying on the floor three feet from me.

I was just stuck in my head, breathing heavily.

I don't know how long I sat there in a daze before going over to the cashier.

I knelt beside him.

I was a Pre-Med student. We'd gone over protocol for everything: what to do when someone didn't have a pulse, how to wrap an injury, and how to stop a patient from bleeding out. We'd gone through it all.

But nothing came to mind.

I had no idea how to help him.

There was blood on his shirt.

Blood on his nametag.

His name was Dan.

. . .

A blanket hugged my shoulders as I sat in the back of the ambulance. The sun faded, and darkness overtook the sky by the time Andy got there.

Andy didn't even turn off his car before running to me.

"Oh my god, are you okay?" He looked me over, trying to find injuries. But there were none.

I wasn't the one who got hurt.

"They took him away," I said.

"Who?"

He didn't know the details. The cops were called by

someone who was walking by when the robber ran from the store. I guess the pedestrian heard gunshots and called the police.

When they came, I was in the same spot, sitting by his body.

He was dead by the time they got there.

One of the police gave me a look, like they knew I didn't try to help him.

I wondered if they were disappointed I didn't save him.

"Dan," I told Andy.

They took him away. They put a sheet over his pale, dead eyes, and they took him away.

There was a man who stole.

A man who died.

And a Pre-Med student who did nothing to help.

i don't learn anymore
December 8

I sat in my class, staring at the pages of my textbook. None of the information reached my mind.

My professor was talking, and all I could think about was how useless it all was. I knew the protocol, but it didn't help me when I was actually in a life-or-death situation.

I looked around, trying to figure out which of my classmates were cut out for this.

I wasn't, that was for sure.

Maybe she'd be able to deal with it, but definitely not him.

I started picking people apart, left and right, comparing myself to them all.

What would they have done?

I started to notice the ones who were just putting up a front, pretending they were ready when deep down, they knew their hands would shake too much when inspecting a patient, that their compressions wouldn't be deep enough, not fast enough to save a life.

I could spot the ones who were afraid to break ribs.

But I also saw those who had a different drive, something in their nature that made them capable of handling more than the average person. The ones who could see patients die right in front of them and not die along with them.

How did I not see it before?

nightmares take a toll
December 20

Every night I had the same dream.

It was the man from the gas station.

It started with a knock at the door. I was in my dorm room, and I went to answer it. I opened the door, and there he was.

He stood in front of me, dead eyes locked onto mine.

I screamed for help as he stepped toward me, his expressionless face twisting into a bitter rage.

"You did this!"

He stepped closer to me, and I backed away. Step after step until I was against the wall of my dorm, nowhere else to run.

"You did this!"

Over and over until I dropped to my knees.

That's when I would wake up.

I woke up completely drenched in sweat. I could never tell if it was sweat or tears all over my face, but I was pretty sure it was tears that night. I kicked off all the sheets in a panic, still half in the dream world.

But a hand grabbed my shoulder, stopping me dead in my tracks.

At least tonight, I didn't scream when I saw Hillary.

Two nights ago, I screamed and woke up some of the students in nearby dorms. They knocked on the door to see what had happened. Hillary talked to them, and now, they gave me sympathetic looks whenever I passed them.

The night before that, Hillary had to call Andy so he could calm me down.

"It's just me," Hillary said.

She looked so vulnerable in the middle of the night. She was always invincible during the day, with her dark eyeshadow and her leather boots. Hillary always looked like she was ready for a fight, even though she was the best friend I'd ever had.

At night, though, she looked like the rest of us.

Scared and unprepared.

"It's just me," she repeated.

She handed me the glass of water at my bedside.

She didn't ask me what the dream was about. It had been the same ever since that day. The same nightmare over and over.

Hillary gave me a sleeping pill I got from the doctor, and I took it begrudgingly. I didn't like taking pills because I was scared I'd become addicted. Sometimes little red flags go off, alerting you of a potential snare, and when I looked at those pills, I knew they'd get the better of me if I let them.

Hillary made me take them, though, most nights. She said the doctors gave me them for a reason. She was right, but I was still skeptical.

Within ten minutes, I was asleep.

cartoon afternoons
January 3

When I was little, I was always trying to show off in front of our neighbor. He was four years older than me and always seemed so cool. So, I'd ride my bike up and down our street, trying to do new tricks and impress him.

But I always fell.

He wouldn't help me when I hit the ground. I'd have scrapes and bruises all over, and he would just watch me struggle to get off the road.

He watched me like I was just entertainment- a performance he found amusing.

What would she try next?

I think he pretended he was in a different reality than me. He never helped me when I wanted him to.

One time, I was flung off my bike, and I skidded down the hill. My whole leg, ankle to thigh, was completely shredded. There was blood everywhere.

But I walked my bike back up my driveway, blood dripping down my leg into my sock.

We made eye contact that day, and I saw him falter. It dawned on him that maybe one day I'd be really hurt, and perhaps he'd be at fault for not helping.

I kept walking, trying to look triumphant even though my legs were burning like a thousand suns.

I got inside, and Mom's mouth dropped open.

"Stop doing those nasty tricks," she said.

Mom sat me in front of the TV so I could watch cartoons while she cleaned my scrapes. And just like that, everything was fixed.

That was how Mom solved everything when we were little. She'd put us by the TV, and we watched the dots on the screen until everything was magically fixed.

I didn't remember the pain I felt when she used peroxide

to clean the wounds, even though I must have felt it.

Now, things weren't so simple. Not after what I did at the gas station.

I couldn't turn on the TV and forget all the pain I felt, all the guilt that weighed me down.

I wished I could go back to that time when cartoons so easily solved my problems.

I wondered when the healing properties of cartoons ended. I wondered when we started to outgrow all the coping mechanisms that worked so well.

Because now, I didn't have a clue how to distract myself from the pain.

the crash
January 6

"Your mom called to make sure we're still planning to video chat with her tonight," Andy said into the phone.

We didn't go back home for Winter Break. I should have, but I didn't want June or Griffin to see me like this.

It was hard enough to rehash everything over the phone when it happened.

"I'll call."

"I'm not saying you *have* to call her," he said. There was a tone of annoyance in his voice. "I'm just asking because she wanted me to ask you. I'm not trying to add anything to your plate."

"Did I say you were?"

I'd been short with him lately. I was trying to be better about it, but it wasn't working.

"No, but you're acting like it."

"Well, I'm not. You can tell my mom I'll call her. Thanks for being the messenger."

"I wouldn't have to be if you'd answer your messages."

"I would call her back if you all would give me a *second*."

There was a pause.

"Fine. Call her yourself."

"Fine."

I slammed my hands on the steering wheel and started the car.

I drove until I had no idea where I was. I was out on some open road, going who knows where, and I was panicking. It was the panic that settled deep in your chest and suffocated you until you couldn't breathe.

And I was sitting there, every muscle in my body completely tight, pressing my foot down on the gas pedal until I couldn't push anymore.

There was a certain medley playing, like the whir of the wheels was playing me a song.

I liked the tune, so I kept going.

There was a slight turn in the road, and as I flew through it, I realized how easy it would be for me to crash.

Crash and end it all.

I was going so fast, there'd hardly even be any pain.

The medley kept singing, and my chest kept heaving, and there was a way out.

It was right there, right at my fingertips.

It would be so easy.

I remembered when my grandma's friend died. Mom told me about her, and I said I was sorry to hear that. But I went about my day unaffected because people die every day, and people live on every day.

I wondered if I would be the type of person whose death people were unaffected by.

I wondered if they'd say how sorry they were and then go right back to texting their friends or scrolling through social media without giving me a second thought.

It would be so easy.

My hands gripped the steering wheel, and I was ready to do it- spin the car and make it fly over the barricade on the right side.

It was so easy.

Andy said everything was hard nowadays. Not this, though. This would be the easiest thing I'd ever done.

But Andy.

The thought of him shook me to my core.

Andy.

Andy was waiting for me at the dorm. We were supposed to have dinner tonight.

I wanted to be there for him. I did.

What was I thinking, trying to throw my car off a cliff while Andy was waiting for me?

Without thinking, I slammed on my brakes.

The car skidded before it flipped.

. . .

When I came to, I was on my side, the whole world tilted to the side. The sunroof window was shattered, and I struggled to crawl out of it onto the street.

Glass cut into my hands and knees. There was blood on my clothes.

My pretty clothes.

The shirt June got me was spotted with red.

When I made it to the street, I started to freak out. It took me a while to calm down enough to think properly.

I paced in front of the totaled car.

How stupid could I be?

What was wrong with me?

This is what I got for everything I'd done. The world was punishing me. It wanted me dead that night.

I saw my phone lying on the ground inside the car, and I reached in, pulling the phone out. I held it in my hands so gently, like it would shatter if I mishandled it.

"Hey," Andy answered when I called. "Are you on your way to the dorm?" When I didn't reply, his voice got deeper, softer. "What's wrong?"

"I'm sorry," I choked out. "I messed up."

"Are you hurt?"

"It's just a wreck," I said. But I didn't answer the question.

He didn't waste any time. "Where are you?"

I had no idea where I was. I must have taken too long figuring it out because Andy didn't wait for a response.

"It's fine. I'll just track your phone. Okay? I'll be there as soon as I can. I'm going to stay on the line with you."

I nodded as if he could see me.

He talked on the phone for a long time while I sat on the road next to the jacked-up car. He told me not to worry, and that he was craving pizza, and that he'd get me whatever food I wanted if I'd just hang in there. He was stalling, talking nonsense just to make sure I didn't run off and do anything worse.

He was a good rambler, always had been. He was born for a situation like this.

His consistent flow of words took my mind off the slice in my arm.

Andy pulled up and ran toward me, his mouth dropping open when he saw the totaled car.

"My god, Beck," he breathed.

But it only took him a second before he locked his attention on me.

I burst into tears as soon as I saw him. I felt guilty for everything. For thinking how easy it would be to leave him.

"I could have done it," I sobbed.

He pulled me into his arms before I could even finish the sentence. He was trying to calm me down, but I just kept talking, repeating my apologies.

Surely, he couldn't actually make out what I was saying; my crying words were all jumbled up.

But he kept reassuring me as if he could understand every syllable. Maybe he could.

"Come on, let's get you home."

That night, when he took me to my room and put a blanket over me, I wasn't worried about the totaled car. I knew he'd take care of it all.

Andy would take care of everything.

It just made me cry harder.

I told him about my grandma's friend and how she died, and how I felt nothing even though I probably should have. I told him that people die, and everyone forgets about them.

"Sure, you don't matter to a lot of people," Andy said when I finished my spiel that was broken up by sobs. "But there are always people who will lose their whole world if you die. And that's what keeps you around."

the dropout
February 7

"There's no other option?" Mom asked.

I shook my head even though I knew she couldn't see me through the phone. Andy sat on the bed beside me, resting against the headboard. I had the call on speakerphone. "I've done everything I can, but it's just not working."

There was a pause. I knew Mom didn't want me to leave college, but she understood the problems I was facing, too.

"You leave with the intent to return," June reminded Mom. June did a lot of research on leaves of absence.

"Do you? Intend to return?" Mom asked me.

"Ideally, yes," I said. "I'll have the semester off and see where I'm at over summer."

"That seems reasonable," Dad said. I knew he was saying it for Mom's sake more than mine.

She clicked her tongue. "I just don't want you to mess up your life with this."

"If anything, this is what's going to save my life, Mom."

Andy squeezed my leg.

"What does Andy think about it?" Mom asked.

She always liked hearing Andy's opinions; she trusted what he had to say.

"She's doing the right thing," Andy said to the phone. "It's a good decision. I trust her."

"I've already turned in the papers, Mom. There's nothing else I can do. It was getting so bad, even with the medicine. I just want a break to focus on myself. I need a break. I need this so bad, Mom."

I knew she didn't like thinking about the night of the car crash. Andy called her that night when he thought I was asleep. I couldn't hear what she said, but I could hear how he tried to calm her down. I knew she was crying on the other end.

"Then, good for you."

She said it shortly, almost sternly, but I knew she wasn't upset. Mom knew this was the best decision for me. She just didn't want to give up her college dream.

She told all her friends how her oldest daughter was a first-generation college student and a soon-to-be doctor! Now she'd have to take it all back.

"When are you coming home?" Dad asked hopefully.

That was the part I'd been shying away from. I knew they'd support me about taking the leave of absence and dropping Pre-Med.

Me not coming home, though? That was a whole different story.

"I'm staying here." I tried not to wince as I said it.

"Why aren't you coming home?" June asked. Her voice was hurt.

It was because I chose Andy. Andy was my home now, and I needed him.

I felt a little guilty about it when I first made up my mind to stay in Boston. But wasn't that what happened when you fell in love?

You left your family to start a new one.

As hard as it was for me, I knew Andy was who I needed to get me through this.

"I'm staying here because Andy's been a huge help," I answered honestly. "I have a whole support system over here, and I just don't want to leave yet."

It was like I betrayed them.

"You're coming back for Spring Break, right?" June asked.

"Of course. And I'll be there all summer."

"Okay, fine," she said. "But you owe me big time."

I laughed. There was my June Bug.

the echoes of empty rooms
February 9

My dorm was all packed up. I'd rolled up my posters, stacked my CDs, and wrapped my mugs and teapots. They were all in boxes that Andy and Paul took down to the car.

Hillary sat on her bed, looking at the empty side of the dorm. She was wearing a new band tee, and she fiddled with her fishnets.

"I'm probably gonna get a crackhead for a roommate. Or

a serial killer. If I end up washed up or dead, know it's your fault," she said.

Hillary had been bitter ever since I told her I was moving.

"Okay, that'll be on me," I smiled.

"You better come hang out," she said with a pointed finger. She looked sad.

"Of course, I will. Besides, you have a concert next week, and there's no way I'm missing it," I assured her.

But the truth was, it felt like I was moving far, far away. In reality, the apartment was only five miles away, but it seemed like we'd be millions of towns apart.

Hillary didn't look convinced, so I walked over and hugged her. It was easy to believe we'd stay in touch as we held each other. And I really hoped we would.

Andy came back to the room and paused in the doorway. "Whenever you're ready," he said.

I nodded.

"See you next week," I told her.

"See you next week. At the front, screaming the loudest."

We both smiled at that, thinking back to when she and the band got their first gig. It seemed like ages ago.

I left with Andy, and it took us only a few minutes to get to my apartment.

I took the key out of my pocket and opened the front door, swinging it open to reveal this big, open room with a counter by the kitchen and a little hallway that led to the bathroom. When we stepped inside, our footsteps echoed.

The metal key was in my hand; I squeezed it so hard that it made an imprint on my skin.

I was starting over.

And I suddenly felt like this wasn't the right option anymore. Maybe I should have gone home after all. It would have made more sense than this.

"How are you doing?" Andy asked, coming up behind me and wrapping his arms around my waist.

That was exactly why I didn't go back home. Because he was what kept me grounded nowadays, and I didn't want to see what I'd be without him.

"It'll be good," I said, nodding to increase my conviction.

"That's not what I asked, Beck. How are you holding up?"

I turned to face him, his arms still around me.

"Honestly? I'm just tired."

"Of what?"

"Of thinking about what's wrong," I told him. "We've been so worried about everything, trying to figure out the future even though we have no control over it. And I think it's driving us both crazy."

"Let's take it one day at a time, then. We've got forever to worry about the future."

"I like the sound of that," I said.

He kissed me, and everything was good again. It all seemed so simple when he did that. With one look, he could take away all my fears.

Paul cleared his throat, and Andy and I separated to look at him. "There are boxes downstairs, you know," he said, his arms full of boxes.

"That's what you're here for!" I teased. But I put my hands in my back pockets and leaned away from Andy. He sighed, and his grasp on me left as we walked to help Paul unload the car.

. . .

We sat on the floor (because there was only one chair we'd assembled so far), and we played video games. It was the three of us, with old game controls plugged into the TV.

Andy and I used to have video game all-nighters, but we hadn't done that in a long time.

I remembered how much I missed it.

Eventually, I let him and Paul play while I rested my head in Andy's lap.

The sound of them collecting coins was oddly soothing, and I started drifting off. I knew I'd be sleeping with a smile on my face that night.

isolation
February 12

I was glad Jamie still let me work at the record store with reduced hours because I was completely isolated without school and my friends. I didn't like the person I was when I was by myself.

Thankfully, Jamie accommodated my schedule, letting me work minimum hours, giving me enough space not to feel overwhelmed but still giving me an escape from the apartment and myself.

I watched a lot of movies during the day, watching the TV until my eyes burned.

I called Isaac to check on him. He said his father was doing good and that he was happy to be back home with him. He seemed to be doing alright.

When Isaac asked how I was, I lied and said I was doing good.

When we hung up the phone, I went back to my movies and cried myself to sleep.

this is why you shouldn't eavesdrop
February 19

I got to his dorm room with gifts of dessert in my hands. I made a pie for him- lime, just like he liked.

He was going to be studying all night. There was a big exam the following day he was stressed about.

I was about to knock on the door when I heard someone say my name from inside.

Eavesdropping wasn't polite. I knew that.

When I was younger, Mom always got on my case because I loved listening to conversations that weren't mine.

I liked hearing the hushed tones when my parents had little arguments.

I liked hearing my sister tell my mom a secret her teddy bear told her.

I liked picking up pieces of conversations and feeling like I was a part of them.

But now, the conversation *was* about me. I was dying to know what they were saying, so I ignored the way my guilty conscience pulled me away, and I pressed my ear against the door.

"Don't get me wrong, Rebecca is great." It was Paul's voice. "I love her, and I love her with you. But she's got a lot of issues she has to work out herself."

I really liked Paul. We'd gotten close after hanging out for the past year. I knew he was my friend, but his loyalty would always be with Andy. And honestly, he wasn't wrong.

Andy spoke defensively. "Hey, she's doing fine."

His voice didn't sound confident.

"I see the way you take a few minutes to relax after you get off the phone with her. Like she drains you or something."

Was that true? Did I drain all the life out of him?

"That's not true," Andy protested. There was a pause.

It was because he had to mature so much to take care of me. As much as I'd like to tell myself: *No, you haven't ruined him*, my gut was telling me otherwise.

"I just get worried about her sometimes. For the most part, we're good. We get each other through everything."

I was all panicky, waiting for him to finish his thought. What was he going to admit? What would he say about me when he thought I was out of earshot?

"But sometimes it's just hard. She takes her mind with her, and I can't help her. No one can."

My breath was heavy against the door.

"What are you gonna do?"

"What can I do? I just have to be there, I guess. Be there and hope it's enough."

It was like a hammer to my chest. I felt it in my bones, that desperate, starving hope that strangled us both. We were just hoping things would be okay.

We saw all the red signs, and we slammed on the gas to keep going.

We were going to be blindsided by it all one day.

Eventually, we were going to wish we would've hit the brakes.

our care packs
February 25

June liked sending me care packs every month. I think she was the one who made Mom and Dad send them in the first place. The boxes were full of things only she'd think to send, even though the whole family always signed the notes.

When I opened the care pack, there was a box of honey cereal with a little sticky note that said to eat it with bananas.

I had assured her we had the same cereal in Boston, but June said it was nice knowing we were eating from a box bought from the same store. I think it made her feel closer to me, knowing she had the box that was right next to mine in the aisle. Knowing she touched it and paid for it and sent it.

I never brought up the logistics again.

I liked that she kept sending it.

There were also a bunch of candles inside, with a letter telling me about how she started her own candle-making company on a crafty website she was obsessed with.

I was happy to see she put my scent mixture recommendations to good use. And the money I lent her.

I went through the rest of the box.

There was a cat teacup that she wrapped in newspaper.

She packed some chewy fruit candies from the Korean grocery store.

There was a purple silk top that June had found at a thrift shop. I wore silk clothes like Andy wore sweaters. Every time June saw one, she would send it to me.

The family wrote out a message. All of them wrote down something to say; four times, the handwriting changed.

When it got to Griffin's part, he said he had new comic books he would let me borrow when I visited for Spring Break.

That was as close to an "I love you" as he ever got. He must have really missed me that month.

I loved receiving my care packages. It was something simple, but it brought me so much joy to receive a little bit of home with each box. No matter what was happening in my life, I felt safe when I got that care pack.

My family was back at home, but they were still watching out for me. I would always have them, no matter how far away I was.

Andy didn't get care packages from his family. He got one the first month we were together, right after his parents had told him about the divorce.

His care package was just a sweater and a watch that he'd left at home. There was also a ticket to Seattle.

It was so weird to me how unfriendly his box was.

Mine were things that would remind me of home; his were things that would help him start a life away from it.

But that was the difference between us.

Andy wasn't raised in a house that felt like home. Home was just temporary for him, a place he took with him wherever he went.

I don't think he ever intended to stay in Boston. He wanted to study abroad and leave whenever he could.

Two years ago, he picked the farthest place to run away from his parents. But times changed, and now he was going even farther.

I kept thinking about his application to Cambridge. I dreaded the day when I'd have to say goodbye.

Andy would be accepted. And he wouldn't hesitate to go; he was dying to take off again.

Pack up and take home with him.

Meanwhile, I was still trying to make a life for myself in Boston, even though I knew my real home would always be that old house in Cali.

cambridge
February 28

I thought having my own apartment would make things easier. I figured it would give me some space, give me some time to figure things out by myself.

But as the nights passed with me bawling on the couch, I

realized it wasn't such a good idea after all.

The panic attacks came out of nowhere. One moment I'd be completely fine, and the next, I wasn't. I was freaking out, and everything was spinning, and I was falling apart. The migraines were so bad that the medicine hardly even helped.

The doctors said it was PTSD.

Really, though, it was just guilt.

Guilt rotted my insides and ate me alive until I wanted to die.

There were knocks at the door, and I pulled myself upright to answer. My shaking hands wiped the tears from my face.

I paused at the mirror before I answered. I knew it was Andy coming to see me.

He had a special knock ever since he found out about my nightmares. He knew I didn't like opening the door if I didn't know who it was.

I was paranoid, thinking there was going to be another incident. It was something I'd been dealing with since it happened.

Looking in the mirror, I realized how well I cleaned up. My eyes were still a little red, my lashes still damp, but I hoped he wouldn't notice. I hoped he wouldn't see all my tremors, all my tells.

When I opened the door, Andy greeted me with a huge smile on his face. But immediately, the smile disappeared, and worry overcame his face.

He could see right through me.

Andy closed the door behind us as he touched my face.

"If I knew you were going to spend all your time crying alone, I never would have gotten you the apartment," he said.

I waved him off.

"What were you going to tell me?" I asked, turning away from him, trying to sound as cheery as I could. I didn't want him worrying about me all the time. I knew it was taking a toll on him.

"Nothing," he said with a shrug.

"Come on. What were you going to say?" I repeated. But really, I already knew the answer. I already knew he'd been accepted before he said a word.

I wondered when we got this way, anticipating everything the other one did. I wondered if that was what being an old married couple was like. If we were able to know each other's thoughts after not even two years, what would it be like after fifty years? Maybe it was comforting to know someone through and through. Perhaps it was safe that way.

But maybe it was exhausting, having two people's thoughts in your head all the time.

"Well," Andy said, still worried about me. "I wanted you to be the first to know I got accepted!"

I flung my arms around him.

"That's amazing!" I exclaimed. "I'm so proud of you!"

He breathed out low. "It's...wild. I can't believe it."

"I can. You're a genius. The space field needs more

people like you."

And it was true. Ever since I'd met Andy, this was his dream. This was what he'd wanted for as long as I'd known him. Cambridge had one of the best programs in the world, even if it was the farthest from home.

"You're happy for me?" He asked it like he needed confirmation.

"Of course, Andy." My eyebrows pulled together. Had I given him a reason to doubt that I wanted him to succeed? "Why wouldn't I be?"

He shook his head like it was nothing.

I was hurt he even had to ask.

"I was just worried about me going to another country next semester. Like, are you going to be okay? How is this going to work?" Andy asked. "I mean, if there's any part of you that wants me to stay here, I will. I can turn it down if you want. I just...I know we're in a delicate place right now, and I don't want to jeopardize this. I want *this*. *You're* what I want."

He spoke fast.

I shook my head. "There's always going to be a part of me that wants you to stay here with me. I'm selfish like that."

He smiled.

"But," I continued, "You should go. You deserve this."

Andy looked sad, like he was anticipating something bad. Like he knew something I didn't.

"This won't ruin us?" he asked.

I had to control the hesitation in my voice because I knew

if he picked up on it, he'd stay here with me. And I didn't want that.

"We'll be fine," I said.

Truly, I didn't know if we'd be fine. I was having doubts of my own because I couldn't imagine being apart from him. Wasn't that why I was here and not back at home? Wasn't that the reason he set me up at this apartment once I took my leave from college? Because we were afraid to be apart from each other? Because we were scared if we put distance between us, we'd both fall apart and be unrepairable?

How would Andy going to Europe be any different?

But I knew I'd have to pretend it would be for his sake. I didn't want him to give up his dreams because of my issues. This is what he wanted. This is what he needed to do.

"Thanks, Roo," he said, kissing my cheek. "I'm so excited! If I can make my mark over there, I might be recruited. I could actually be creating rockets that send people into space. I could be part of a whole new generation that's going to explore space like never before!"

I bet he was right. I bet he would be someone you'd see on TV in ten years when they discovered a new galaxy or sent astronauts to some never-before-seen planet.

He wouldn't be the one everyone talked about, of course- the astronauts would receive the praise.

But Andy would be the genius behind the operation. The one who made it possible.

I had no question about that.

"Then you'll be the coolest guy in the whole galaxy," I said, smiling cheesily.

"Look who's the dork now," he said, laughing.

"Nope, that's still you," I teased.

And we were on the couch, laughing hysterically, messing around, and being silly. It was like when you were a kid and made a new friend, and within a couple of hours, you'd be holding hands, and play-fighting, and acting like you'd known each other your whole life. That was how it felt with him.

I was just then seeing a new side of him that I hadn't seen in forever. I was meeting him for the first time again, and instantly, we were best friends.

There was no baggage between us at that moment. It was just us laughing and playing.

I forgot what it was like to not carry around the guilt of someone's blood on your hands. But Andy made me remember what it was like to be a kid again.

the window seat
March 26

I remembered how cold I was on the plane the first time Andy and I flew back to California for Winter Break.

Now it wasn't so cold. Now it was spring, and we were used to flying back on our breaks.

We had a schedule now. Andy took the luggage and packed the neck pillows. I had gum in my purse for him because his ears popped when we were up so high. I had our movies downloaded and ready to watch. Last year, I bought an adapter so we could both listen with our own headphones. Andy let me take the window seat, and he asked the flight attendant for chocolate candy and soda for me.

It was a good system.

We each had our strengths. We each took care of certain things and left the rest for the other. It hadn't failed us yet.

But this time, we were boarding the plane, and he didn't let me go down the aisle first.

He took the window seat.

He was ruining the system. Now, I would have to tell the flight attendant what we wanted. And that was a problem because he changed his mind all the time. Sometimes he wanted peanuts, and sometimes it was pretzels; sometimes he wanted a drink, and sometimes he didn't.

How would he lean over me and point out all the things he pointed out every time we flew?

"What's wrong, Beck?" he asked, settling in his seat.

I knew I was going to sound spoiled if I told him I wanted the window seat. I always got the window seat, I realized that. But I wasn't used to him changing it up on me.

It was nothing. But it felt like everything.

It was just one more change in the ever-changing shift between us.

240

It just solidified how I'd been feeling for the past few months, that he was changing, and *we* were changing. It wasn't the same dynamic we used to have.

And it scared me.

"You okay?" he asked, repeating his concern.

I swallowed. "Yeah."

But it wasn't okay. Andy didn't ramble like he used to; he didn't get nervous anymore. I didn't laugh or party like I used to.

There was a problem, a distance separating us.

I wondered if he sensed it too.

I sat down in the not-window seat, certain that things weren't right between us.

the walkout
March 29

I never understood brunch. I didn't see the appeal of it. Eat in the morning and eat in the afternoon; why did they smash them into one awkwardly timed meal?

But middle-aged white ladies always seemed to love brunch.

So, it came as no surprise to me when Carlotta set up a brunch date for our two families.

She made a reservation for the café by the beach for 10:30. She reserved the second level just for us. Like the seven of us really needed an entire restaurant floor.

But the materialistic part of myself kind of liked having a boyfriend with so much money that he could reserve restaurants on a whim.

Andy's parents did this a lot, throwing cash to make their problems go away.

It didn't actually work, but it made everything seem a lot cooler in the process.

That side of Andy came out when he was around his mother. Back in the dorms, he never made a fuss about expenses. You'd never even know he was from a wealthy family. But as soon as Carlotta was around, he looked for ways to blow cash. Something in him, no matter how much he rebelled against it, would always be his mother's son.

I came back home from my morning coffee run, and before I even opened the front door, I could hear the booms and bangs of an action movie.

The melody of violence greeted me as I stepped inside.

Griffin and Andy were sitting on the couch, watching a movie in nearly identical poses. They leaned forward in anticipation, hands on knees. They both turned toward me at exactly the same time, superhero masks made out of paper plates concealing their faces.

It was so cute how well Griffin and Andy got along. Almost every time we came back, the two of them had a superhero movie marathon. They'd be glued to the screen for the entire day, bonding over doing nothing.

I remembered how easily Andy won over my family the first time he met them. Griffin practically idolized him; when I video-chatted the family from college, he asked more about Andy than he did me.

"Hey guys," I said, putting the keys down and joining them on the couch.

"Shhh," Griffin criticized. "This is the part where the villain shows up."

"When did you stop by? I didn't know you were coming over," I told Andy in a hushed tone so I wouldn't disrupt Griffin's movie watching.

"Like, thirty minutes ago. I wanted to hang out before we have to go to the Momster's brunch." He kept on his superhero mask, but I knew he was rolling his eyes. "My dad will be there too, which should be fun."

I cringed.

Carlotta derived some twisted pleasure from inviting Mr. Bynes to events, even though they were divorced. She got a new boyfriend recently, one that she loved to parade around. It was just another one of the stupid games Carlotta liked to play.

"The brunch of my nightmares," I said.

He tapped my knee with an open palm. "You and me both, Roo."

I didn't want to think about the party Carlotta was throwing in two days. She invited my family and me to one of the famous parties she threw. Carlotta threw parties so often that the motive for the event could never be identified. She claimed this one was a welcome back party for us, but I had my doubts. I didn't need to attend Carlotta's party to know it would be a night filled with passive-aggressive small talk and condescending glares.

Griffin turned toward us and exclaimed, "If you guys are gonna talk during the whole thing, then you can't stay."

Andy held up his hands in surrender.

"You got a mask for me?" I asked my brother.

Without saying a word, he reached over the side of the couch and tossed me a superhero mask. I put it on, and the three of us watched the rest of the movie, pretending we were all heroes ourselves.

. . .

We sat motionless at the table, except for Griffin, who stabbed his bread rolls with knives and made them dance like feet.

Mom gave him a look, and he stopped reluctantly.

Carlotta was sitting next to her new boyfriend, Miguel, who she'd started dating a month ago. He was too young, too handsome to be with someone like her.

And Mr. Bynes apparently thought so too, with the way he was eyeing his ex-wife from across the table with a stern, disapproving look.

The way she showed off Miguel like a trophy drove everyone crazy.

Andy tensed beside me.

"So," Carlotta said in a scheming tone. "Are you going

with Andy when he leaves for Europe?"

There were lipstick stains on her glass.

"She still has school next semester," Andy said before I could answer.

He didn't tell her about my leave of absence.

"Long-distance doesn't usually work for couples. Especially not for ones as fragile as you."

It had been almost two years; it seemed pretty solid to me.

"Fragile?" Andy repeated.

She shrugged and stabbed at her scrambled eggs.

"Miguel," Mom said, trying to change the subject. She knew what would happen if Carlotta kept pressing Andy. It was what happened every time we sat down for a meal together. "What do you do for work?"

"Business," Miguel said, not making eye contact.

I raised my eyebrows and took a huge bite of my croissant. Business? He was so suspicious.

"Business," Mom repeated, nodding like she understood even though she didn't.

"What kind of business?" Dad asked, trying to draw him out.

"I do things people don't want to do themselves," Miguel answered.

I almost choked on my food. I gave Andy a look like *Your mom is dating a hitman*, and he almost smiled at me. I liked when I could make him smile even when he was pissed off. It made me feel victorious. I knew something everyone else didn't- I knew the way to his heart.

"So, you're like, the mafia or something?" Griffin asked.

"That sounds illegal," Mr. Bynes agreed.

Miguel didn't say anything.

Maybe brunches were sort of fun after all. I mean, how often did you get to meet the real-life mafia?

Carlotta kept a hand on his shoulder throughout brunch, eyeing him in a way that made me so uncomfortable, I had to look away.

"Mom," Andy said in a warning tone.

Mr. Bynes was sitting *right there.*

"Rebecca," she said, smiling sweetly to appease her son. "How are you enjoying Pre-Med?"

We all went silent. Everyone but Carlotta- and Miguel, unless his mafia kept tabs on us- knew I dropped Pre-Med for good.

I took a sip of my water, stalling.

I wasn't sure what to say. If Andy didn't tell her already, he didn't want her to know. But the other option was lying.

My family already knew. They knew about the crash, about why I was leaving; they knew it all. And we weren't the type of family that lied.

"I'm dropping Pre-Med," I said shortly.

Andy wasn't happy with my truth.

Carlotta's eyes flashed like a shark, and I immediately regretted telling her.

"You're dropping Pre-Med?" So condescending, as if she

had three degrees in neuroscience or something.

"I already dropped it. I'm on a leave of absence, and I'm still not sure if I want to go back next semester."

I expected Mom to say something, to defend me from the evil woman, but she didn't. I was thankful she didn't buy into Carlotta's schemes.

"You two are quite the pair: Andy, the aerospace engineer, and Rebecca, a know-nothing dropout. How cute!"

"That's my daughter you're speaking ill of," Dad said. He was so formal when he was upset. His eyebrows crossed, and his features squinted tight.

Carlotta waved her hand in the air innocently. "I can't be the only person who sees the problem in this." She looked at my parents. "You'd think you'd want your daughter to be with someone a little more...her own pace. It's shameful to confine your daughter in the shadow of her lover."

June's mouth dropped open.

June was always too polite to talk back to adults, but I could tell she was dying to go off on Carlotta. She'd be ranting for the rest of the day when we got home.

"That's enough!" Mr. Bynes said, slamming his hand on the table.

"Dad, it's fine." Andy held up a hand. He threw his napkin down on his plate and stood up, pushing his chair back with a satisfying squeak. "That's the thing, Mom. I don't have to listen to this anymore. I don't know why I ever did, to begin with."

He talked big and acted like he didn't care about her opinion, but he did care. I think because she was so absurd, he almost trusted her opinion more than he trusted his dad's.

Andy would storm off, just like how he did every time he was with her, but in the end, it was all the same. He would always be her son; she'd always be his mother.

More than that, I knew Andy would try to prove her wrong for the rest of his life. This comment was going to have serious repercussions. I felt it shaking in my bones. He'd spend the rest of Spring Break making sure Carlotta regretted saying anything about our relationship.

I could only imagine how the party would turn out, both of them seeking revenge on the other- trying to prove points that didn't matter. If they treated each other like this in private, I could only imagine how they'd perform for a crowd.

"Come on, Beck," Andy said, holding a hand out for me.

I looked up at him. Andy was so serious, so tense. He locked his jaw, and his eyes were hard and focused. He glanced down at me, my hesitation making him question whether I'd leave with him.

But of course, I'd leave. Where else would I go?

I took his hand and felt his fingers tighten around mine, strong and reassuring that we'd be okay running off.

"Don't leave," Dad said, pleading with us to sit down.

This wasn't how my family did things. When we had issues, we didn't make scenes and storm off. We didn't leave the table when we were upset, certainly not without finishing our food. Certainly not with guests present. If we had a problem, we'd sit there and talk it out. The situation always dissolved soon enough because none of us could hold a grudge.

But the Bynes? They were a whole different story.

They thrived on making drama. They liked how everyone watched them when they fought, and they liked how it felt to walk away from people.

Maybe that was what attracted me to Andy so much.

Knowing he could walk away from everyone but me.

But maybe that was a problem too. When he walked away, I walked away too. And I'd *never* walk away on my own.

"I'll see you at home, Dad," I whispered, apologizing as I wiggled out from between the chairs.

I heard Carlotta make another snide comment to Miguel, but I couldn't make out the words. We were already out the door, and their voices just turned into mumbles. They were dead words trailing after us.

As he led me out of the building, I noticed the thrill in my heart. I liked running away with him, like we were some star-crossed lovers, defying all expectations.

I liked having a boy whisk me away. It made me feel like I had an entourage or something, the way I trailed behind him while he walked right through everything in our path.

But that in itself made me worry. Because maybe Carlotta wasn't so wrong.

I was always in Andy's shadow.

a party to remember
March 31

I knew something bad was going to happen at the party. I could feel it in the way everyone buzzed, the way Andy played with the hem of his shirt more than usual, the way people kept looking around like they were on edge.

Everyone milled through the venue, and I could hear the meaningless chatter of the attendees. It was a welcome home party for us. A thanks-for-coming-back-to-visit-us-during-Spring-Break party.

But I didn't know more than seven people there.

I didn't want to be there at all, especially after what Carlotta said to us. I didn't want to see her patronizing face or the way she pretended to be proud of us even though she wished me and Andy had never gotten together. I didn't want to deal with her.

And apparently, neither did my family, because they grouped together at the opposite end of the room, as far away as they could get from Carlotta, who made her way through the crowd, smiling with her new boyfriend at her side.

That wasn't how I wanted to spend my night.

But Carlotta never gave me much of a choice. And I wondered what trick she had up her sleeve for tonight. More payback for what Andy did at brunch?

It made my skin crawl, anticipating what could happen. It made me want to run away and not come back.

It was a gorgeous venue, though; I'd give that to Carlotta. The far wall was all glass, and it looked out over the California cliffs. The beach was in the distance, and green hills surrounded us.

The glass reflected the fairy lights hung up across the ceiling.

I caught a glimpse of my silhouette in the reflection, my green, silk spaghetti strap dress gathering in all the right places. It built my confidence to see myself there. Through the frosted mirror, it almost looked like I fit in.

I was even holding a glass of champagne in my hand, the glasses that were long and slender, elegant in their slim form.

Mom styled my hair in an extravagant braid crown, and it was the prettiest I'd ever looked. Wisps of hair framed my face, accenting my features.

In the glass, I saw Andy approach me. I still jumped when he touched my hip, though. I was constantly on edge, paranoid about everything.

My doctor said the medication could do that to me. I thought it would go away after a while, but it never did.

"Hey," Andy greeted me, kissing my neck.

I turned to face him. "Hey, babe."

He looked so good in that suit. He didn't look lanky when he dressed up, and the black jacket made his pale skin look flawless.

But there was a nervousness in his eyes, and it unsettled me.

It scared me when he seemed off. It made me feel like everything was about to go horribly wrong. He was the one who had things together, he was the solid one.

If he worried, I'd be freaked out all day.

I could already feel my anxiety pressing in on me.

"Everything okay?"

I almost didn't want to know the answer.

I felt like everyone was watching us, but I think I was just being paranoid. Everything felt heavy, uneasy, even though nothing was wrong. It was just me getting in my head. It was just me being unsure of everything.

I had felt like that for a while. It was something I hadn't been able to shake since that night.

After the crash, I didn't trust myself. And if I couldn't trust myself, who could I trust?

"Everything's great," he said. But there was something else, something even he wasn't sure of. His hands were on my hips, and his voice was low and quiet. "This past year has been...it's been a chaotic year. It's probably been one of the hardest years of my life. And I've been trying to figure out how to make this year better. I've gone through all these lists, trying to figure it out. And the only thing I can come up with is to keep you in my life."

I was thinking of that night when he drove me home, one hand on the wheel and one hand on my leg as I broke down.

Don't cry. Not now. Not when your makeup is done up so pretty.

I kept telling myself those things, trying to talk myself out of a panic.

"Beck, I don't want this ever to change. I want it to be you and me forever," he said, his lips against my cheek as we swayed to the music.

"Is that too much to ask for?" I asked with a smile. There were tears in my eyes still, but I wouldn't let him see.

Andy shook his head.

And then he got down on one knee.

This was the moment. That moment that kids think about when they're little. It seemed so far off to us back then, but there I was, living it.

My boyfriend was down on his knee, holding a ring in his fingers, asking me to love him unconditionally. This was exactly what I had always wanted. This was exactly how I wanted things to go with Andy.

But now that it was actually happening, I realized how uncertain I felt—blindsided, for sure.

"Rebecca," he said wistfully.

He wasn't doing it right. I could see it in his eyes, the way he was a little distracted, the way he kept glancing over at the glass wall to see the people in the reflection. He was doing it all for show.

He wasn't proposing because he felt that now was the right time, he was proving something.

He was proving it to Carlotta. This was the revenge he had in mind.

It wasn't her I should have worried about that night; it was Andy.

He played a wild card, and I never saw it coming.

"Will you marry me?"

All eyes were on me.

I had to say yes.

I loved him. It was as simple as that. At least, it should have been.

But if it was that simple, why was I having trouble getting out the word?

I remembered the conversation I'd overheard between him and Paul barely even a month ago. I wanted to scream at him that I knew what he said. If that was how he felt, why were we doing this?

But that wasn't important. What was important was that one word.

Yes.

Say yes, Rebecca.

I loved him, and I needed him. What would I do without him?

I couldn't say no. I couldn't humiliate him in front of all these people. I couldn't ruin all that we had.

"Yes!" I exclaimed.

Andy's face relaxed in relief. I'd done it. I was his, and he was mine.

I saw Carlotta's eyes on us, seething at what her son had just done. He was chained to me now, and she couldn't stand it.

Everyone was cheering and clapping. I lifted Andy to his feet, and we kissed.

Even that didn't feel real.

It's like I was in a scene. It was staged, and it wasn't right, and I didn't feel good. But I should have felt like I was on top of the world, because I was with Andy Bynes, and that was all that mattered.

I smiled, and he smiled, and we turned toward the crowd who clapped and took pictures. His breaths were even, so relaxed now. He thought the hard part was over, but all I could think of was how it was only the beginning.

the chasm of sisters
April 1

I had to be at the airport in an hour, but June kept asking me about wedding plans. The party last night filled her head with romance, and it was all she could talk about.

"What sort of cake are you going to have? Red velvet, maybe? I watched a show on wedding planners, and they said red velvet is the sexiest cake you can pick," she said.

I was still packing my suitcase. I was so good at waiting until the last minute.

"Why would anyone want a sexy cake?" I asked, making a face.

"What about your dress? Do you know what kind of dress you're going to wear?"

I shook my head. "I'm not sure." I was still trying to wrap my head around it all.

The ring on my finger still took me by surprise.

It had only been twelve hours.

"*I* know what kind of dress I'm going to wear when I get married," June said excitedly. "One of those ball gowns, with the full bottom. It makes you look like a princess, and it's *so* romantic, don't you think?"

I remembered the champagne bubbles from last night. And I remembered how the chandelier twinkled. And then there was me, in the pretty green dress with a fake smile painted on my face.

It was funny the things that stood out to me on the night I got proposed to.

"Are you listening, Rebecca?" June asked. I nodded. "Opal says when she and Joshua get married, she's going to wear something short and boho. She doesn't even think she wants her dress to be white."

"Hmm," I said while I folded Andy's orchid tie-dye sweatshirt. I wanted to wear it on the plane.

"I mean, it's not like they have a date in mind or anything. They're only sixteen, but they're planning to get married when they're eighteen. I used to think that was sort of young, but you're only nineteen, so it's not that far off. They're so sure of their love that they're already making plans. Isn't that romantic?"

There was a pause, and then June screamed as loud as she could.

It was this high-pitched *shriek* that scared the crap out of me.

I spun to face her, surely looking as shocked as I felt.

"Are you okay? What's wrong?"

"What is wrong with *you*? I have to be screaming or dying in a hospital for you to pay any attention to me!" June exclaimed, exasperated.

"That's not true," I said.

"You never ask about Opal and Joshua- they're my best friends, Rebecca!- and you never ask about how school is going, and you never even listen to me when I talk."

The hurt on her face broke my heart. I promised myself that I'd start asking about her more. I would ask about the drama between her friends.

I wondered how much we contributed to someone else's pain without even knowing it. I wondered if June would grow up and feel like she wouldn't amount to more than a disease. What if she spent her life craving the attention she didn't get when she was younger? Maybe she would tie it back to that moment when she screamed at her sister to listen to her for once.

It's the same way I'd been looking back to that afternoon. I could pinpoint the exact second something snapped inside of me. I'd known when I looked into that man's eyes that I'd never be the same again.

He broke me.

I wondered if people blamed me for breaking them.

"I'm sorry," I said lamely. But I meant it.

"I was going to ask to be a bridesmaid, but I don't think I want to hear the answer." June got up to leave my room but paused by the door. "Unless I get sick again before the wedding. Then maybe you'll take pity on me and let me be in it."

Her words were laced with malice.

For the record, she was always my first choice for a bridesmaid.

knives over hearts
April 1

We were on our way to Boston, and my mind was flying faster than the plane.

"Are you sure about this whole thing?" I asked, playing with my wedding ring. I didn't like the way it fit my finger.

"You're having second thoughts?" Andy questioned. His tone was defensive, and I really should have dropped it.

"I just don't know if this is the right time."

"You wait for the right time, and you'll be dead before it ever comes."

Well then.

"That's dramatic," I said, suppressing the urge to roll my eyes.

"I don't know what else to say. We love each other, right? You want me to go off to Cambridge without you? What choice do we have?"

His mom was right. We wouldn't last long-distance. We were barely holding it together as it was.

"I'm just really struggling right now."

"I get that. And I've been there for you as best I can, but I'm struggling too," he said.

The way he said it made my heart ache.

He was playing with a loose thread on his sweater instead of looking at me.

"I know," I said. "So maybe-"

"Don't go there, Beck."

He said it so harshly, so seriously, that it scared me.

"I'm just saying..."

He knew what I was saying, but he refused to listen.

"We're engaged. I don't know why you have to see the bad in everything. We're together, and things are on the come-up. Everyone's happy for us but you, and I don't think you realize how hard that is for me. This is the happiest moment of my life, looking at my soon-to-be-wife. But you're acting like you want to end things, and it's just...I thought you'd be happy with this."

I looked down at my ring again in silence. It looked better with the sun shining on it.

"We're fine. We'll be good, alright?"

He kissed my cheek, pretending it was all better.

You put a band-aid on, and you won't have to look at the wound.

It would work for a while.

But I saw the way he looked at me.

There were knives in his eyes where there used to be hearts.

white as fallen snow
April 21

I took Hillary with me while I went wedding dress shopping. It had been three weeks of Carlotta texting me about the dress, how the price wasn't an issue and how she'd pay for it, and how I shouldn't pick a strapless gown because my boobs weren't big enough to fill it in.

"You should pick the most expensive dress you can find. Swindle her out of all her money," Hillary joked. She was always coming up with ways to steal Carlotta's money.

Hillary didn't know Carlotta. She just really liked the idea of being rich.

"More like trying to find the cheapest," I said with a sigh. "I don't want her holding this over my head forever."

I could already picture it. Any little disagreement, any

argument, and she'd say: *"Let's not forget who paid for your dress."* I could even see her smug face saying it, too, a fake smile stretching her plastic skin across her cheeks, reminding me of her wealth and my lack of it.

Hillary and I went inside a wedding boutique store with a cute little bouquet next to the sign. It looked so sweet, so simple.

I was going to be a bride soon.

It should have made me feel as loving as the scent in the shop.

But I felt like it wasn't right.

A little old woman who worked there came to help us. She had a peachy, whiskery mustache.

"Hi dears," she said. "Which one of you is the bride-to-be?"

She didn't even look at Hillary, though, like she didn't entertain the thought of the platinum blonde girl with black lipstick being bride material.

But maybe it wasn't the way Hillary dressed that made the woman lock onto me. Maybe after working with brides for a while, she could identify the people who were in love.

Suddenly, I was happy she kept looking at me. Maybe she could tell I was in love.

Hillary gestured to me, and I waved my hand.

"Congratulations," the woman said with a smile. Her withered hands clasped together in front of her stomach. "Do you have any style in mind?"

I felt like I was the only person who hadn't had their

wedding dress planned out for years. It wasn't that I couldn't picture myself getting married. I just thought it would be farther in the future. In high school, I was a short-term girlfriend, the kind of girlfriend who broke things off before the six-month anniversary. So, I didn't think I'd find someone serious until further down the road, at least not until after college. I guess I never felt the need to plan for a wedding.

"I don't have anything, in particular, I'm looking for," I said.

"Except no mermaid dresses," Hillary chimed in. She saw this girl walk down the aisle in a mermaid dress once, and the bride tripped. That experience only added to the long list of reasons why mermaid dresses were Hillary's nemeses.

The little old lady gave us a tour through the boutique, pointing out her favorites. She put a few in my arms and ushered me into the dressing room.

Hillary sat on the pastel chair while I changed.

"So, where's your head at?" she asked.

I fiddled with the zipper at my lower back.

"What do you mean?"

"I mean, we haven't talked much since you've come back from Spring Break. Everyone came back with a hangover, and you came back with a ring. That's heavy. How do you feel about it all?" Hillary said.

There was the slightest moment of hesitation before I answered.

"It's a dream come true."

I stepped out of the dressing room and paraded around for Hillary to see. I was unamused by it, and she made a face.

"Try the princess one," she said, and I went back into the changing room. "You don't seem thrilled about this wedding. What's up?"

I didn't want to say it out loud. When you say something, speak it into the universe, it makes it true. I couldn't take it back if I told her.

"Come on, Rebecca. I'm getting bored. What is it?" Her voice was impatient.

"I'm just having a hard time processing it all," I said. That was a start.

"But this is what you want, right? I mean, you love Andy." But the latter part, she said like it was a question, like she doubted my loyalty to him.

I wiggled into the dress.

"I love him. It's just...I don't know how to explain it. It's like, I'm living this happily ever after, but it's not *my* happily ever after. I feel like I'm living out the wrong life or something."

"Who cares if it's the wrong life if you're happy?"

I paused. She had a point.

"I can't figure it out. But I know we're doing this just because it's what we're expected to do. And it feels like a game of chicken. Like, who's going to back out first? But we're too scared of being lonely to call it quits," I said.

I leaned against the dressing room door. I didn't want to go out yet. It was easier talking to someone when you didn't have to see their disappointment.

"You think Andy feels this way too?" Hillary asked.

I could picture her sitting out there, biting her nails in concern.

"In his own way, yes," I confirmed. "He's running around making plans on a whim. Andy's never done that before. We were on a date once, and he took a solid ten minutes to pick out an ice cream flavor. He's the most indecisive person I know. But not anymore. Now he's being spontaneous and jittery, and it all boils down to him freaking out and wanting to run."

There was a pause. "And what's your way of coping with it?"

"The exact opposite. It drains all my energy to think about what this summer has to hold. And I still can't get past everything that happened last fall. It's just so hard. I'm just trying to stay afloat," I said.

"Did you tell Andy that? Maybe it'll help if you told him."

I shook my head and opened the door to face her. "I told him the day after he proposed."

"And what did he say?" she asked.

"He said we didn't have any other options. And honestly, I think he's right. That's what scares me most."

I spun around in the dress, using the white material to distract me from the conversation.

Hillary shook her head. "It looks too middle-aged white lady," she said, commenting on the dress I wore.

"We're never going to find a dress," I groaned.

"It's been *two* tries!" She rolled her eyes. "Go try that other one you picked out."

I did, and when I came out, her jaw went slack.

"Rebecca, that's gorgeous! Do you love it?"

I looked in the mirror. The dress was beautiful; there was no doubt about that. It was a simple, A-line fit with a modest train.

I couldn't wait to see Andy's face when he saw me in it.

Maybe it wouldn't be so bad after all. Maybe it was just major pre-wedding jitters. I just had to get through the next few months, and then we'd be fine.

It was easy to convince myself of that when I was wearing a wedding dress and thinking about his smile.

I took out my phone and snapped a picture. Hillary was in the background, throwing peace signs while I had my tongue out.

"Who are you sending that to?" she asked, laughing. There was only a split second before she caught on. "No, you can't send it to Andy! Don't let him see the dress before the wedding!"

I waved off her concern and texted him the picture anyway.

Almost immediately, he responded with: *I'm smiling so hard right now.*

It was those moments, those texts and words that made me want to stay with him. Andy loved me, and I loved him.

Shouldn't that have been all there was to it?

That had to be enough.

It *had* to.

cry baby
April 23

Andy was so great at taking care of the wedding plans, but I still felt so stressed over the ordeal. I researched the details, looking up articles about tablecloths, centerpieces, and reception decorations. My head was spinning, and I hadn't been able to sleep well for the past few nights because every time I closed my eyes, I saw Andy at the party, proposing to me but not looking me in the eye.

And it just reminded me of everything we needed to do even though our hearts weren't in it.

Andy knocked on the door. Once, twice, once, so I knew it was him. He came into the room, holding binders which I could only imagine were full of magazine cutouts and wedding plans I didn't want to look at.

He set them on the table and took a seat across from me.

"My mom called today to say we need to figure out what kind of catering we want," he said, opening one of the binders. "What are you thinking?"

Catering. Carlotta would disagree with whatever we said

anyway, so why couldn't she just pick?

"Whatever Carlotta thinks will be easiest."

He didn't look happy with that answer. "We can't just let her plan everything. I don't want her having that much control over this. She's already the one paying for it."

He tried to smile, but it didn't catch on.

"I narrowed down the bouquets to these two. So, you can choose," Andy said, flipping a few pages and pointing to the flowers.

"And I've figured out the invites. They look pretty cool, so as soon as you get the guestlist for your side ready, we can send out the invitations."

I breathed out.

"You know how we said dark green, white, and black were going to be the colors? My mom texted me today and said she had a hard time finding green decorations, and she thinks we should change it to red or blush pink, which I'm sure she's only saying because *she* likes those colors. But I wanted to run it by you anyway in case you're having second thoughts about green."

I burst into tears. When I didn't answer, he looked up and saw me bawling like a baby.

"What's wrong?" he exclaimed, closing the binder and moving the chair to sit at my side. "I'm sorry, what's wrong?" His voice was so sweet.

"I'm sorry," I said, leaning my head against his shoulder.

He knew I was burned out before I even said a word. I shouldn't have been crying while I was planning a wedding with my dream guy. I felt so stupid. I was the only girl who couldn't hold it together until after the wedding.

"I'll call my mom back and have her figure out the catering and the bouquets. June can help with the guest list. We'll stick with green."

He was so practical. Even when I was crying, he was figuring out the details.

"I'm sorry," I said again. I was being weak. Stupid and weak.

Andy just sat there, playing with my hair. "It's all good."

the tickets
April 26

Andy came over for movie night just like he did every Thursday night. It had gotten sketchy recently, and we missed a lot of weeks here and there, but tonight he was coming. He picked up Chinese food for us, and when he arrived, he set it down on the table.

He also brought three bottles of beer with him.

He drank more since the party. He never used to drink before.

"Is Hillary coming?" he asked, sitting down on the bed beside me.

Hillary would join us sometimes if it were a movie she

liked. Ever since I moved out of the dorms, she made sure she visited the apartment and hung out with me. She thought we wouldn't stay friends if we weren't living together.

She came over that Thursday, but she left before Andy showed up.

"She's out tonight," I told him. "Her band is playing at some venue downtown."

"I guess that means no murder movies for us tonight," Andy laughed.

Hillary would completely change the movie if she didn't want to leave, which meant we watched many thrillers.

Neither of us liked horror, but Hillary would sit between us while we clung to her in fright. She always claimed she didn't get scared, but she would hesitate before stepping out of my apartment or turning off the light.

"Just cheesy dramas for us," I agreed.

We watched a movie about a high school student who fell in love with a French guy while she was on vacation. I could tell you how it ended even before we clicked play, but at least I wouldn't go to bed scared for the rest of the week.

I popped a huge piece of orange chicken in my mouth, and I chewed on it while I got the movie started.

As I went to hit the play button, Andy stopped me.

"Wait," he said, grabbing my hand.

I looked over at him, my mouth full of the orange chicken wad.

"I have a surprise."

Ever since the gas station, I hated surprises, and he knew it. I stopped chewing.

He leaned over the side of the bed to where his bag was lying on the floor. The sound of him unzipping a pocket filled the silent room. Andy sat back up, showing me the present in his hand.

Two plane tickets.

"Ta-da!" he said. He was smiling. I wasn't.

I took the tickets and looked them over. Two tickets to Cambridge, England. July 30th.

"We can have the wedding, spend the next day together, and then head off to Europe."

It all felt so sudden. I was nauseous.

"Are you excited?" he asked.

Was he oblivious to the pain on my face? I was going to be sick. I breathed through it even though I almost wished I would have just thrown up. Maybe it would have taken away the anxious, paranoid feeling that had paralyzed me for weeks.

"We'll have a month to travel and honeymoon until I start school," he went on.

I would be trailing in his footsteps, standing in the shadows, for the rest of our lives. It would be him calling all the shots from here on out. He'd choose where we went to dinner because he had already visited a cool place when he went to dinner with his classmates. He'd decide how we spent our weekends- if we'd still do our movie night or if we'd be going to a conference.

"I'm giving you a plane ticket to Europe. Why are you acting like this? You're acting like it's the worst thing in the world. This is what you signed up for when you said yes."

He said it in a gruff voice.

"It's just a lot," I said. Part of that was true. Part of me was just having doubts about us in general. But how could I tell him   that?

He was closing off; I could sense it. Andy looked tired before we even started talking. It was preemptive exhaustion.

He crossed his arms and leaned back against the headboard.

"Fine. Just start the movie."

I did, and we watched the movie even though neither of us was paying attention.

call it off
May 5

I sat in Andy's dorm, waiting for him to get back from the engineering room. He and his friends were working late on a project that was part of their final. But by now, they probably finished and were out drinking.

Twenty more minutes passed, and then an hour.

At some point, Paul came in.

"Hey," he said, nodding.

He put on a show for us but left before Andy arrived. He'd been doing that a lot lately, anticipating when Andy and I were going to be arguing. He'd leave before it got awkward.

It was 10:30 when Andy came back to the dorm.

He and his engineering friends came into the room, smiles on their faces. The smile disappeared when he saw me.

It didn't look like he'd been drinking, after all. He looked good, better than I'd seen him look since the party.

I wished that party had never happened.

His dark curls were just messy enough to be hot, he wore an oversized black sweatshirt that hid his lousy posture, and he almost- *almost*- looked genuinely happy.

He started wearing more black after the night of the party, like he was mourning something he hadn't lost yet.

His friends left, and Andy came toward me.

"I didn't know you were waiting for me," he said.

"It's fine," I told him. And honestly, it was. I wasn't there to pick a fight over that.

"Have you eaten? You want me to make dinner?"

"No, I'm not hungry."

There was a long pause as he looked me over, sensing everything was wrong but not knowing exactly what. He looked down at the phone he pulled from his pocket, seeing all the missed calls I'd left him.

I think we should talk tonight.

"Sorry, I didn't see-"

"Andy, I don't think we should do this," I said, cutting

him off before I lost my nerve.

He acted like he didn't know I was going to say that.

"It's not going to work."

He frowned. "Yes, it will. Why won't it?"

I took a deep breath, surprised by his reaction. I thought he'd been thinking the same thing.

"Because," I said. "A friend told me not to marry someone just because you're scared not to. And we're doing this out of fear. I said yes because I was scared. I was too scared to think things through and come up with an answer I didn't like. But you're going to Cambridge next semester, and what? I'm going to be a dropout who's trying to make it in a place that's not my home? I don't want to be in Europe. I don't want to be so far from my family."

He jumped in to defend it all, his eyes desperate. It was all falling out of his control, and he couldn't stand it.

"I've already told you. Come with me to Europe. Take some time for yourself. There's plenty of opportunities there for you. *I'm* there! I'm your fiancé. Don't you see how much fun we'll have in Cambridge?"

I shook my head, and he grabbed my hand.

"Running away isn't going to help this," I said.

"I'm not running away! You say that about everything, like I'm some coward who can't face anything."

"You *do* run from everything. You ran here to get away from your family. And you're running away to Europe to get away from this."

He rolled his eyes and squeezed my hand tight. "I bought *you* a ticket. We're *both* going together. How is that running away?"

I didn't say he was running away from me. I said he was running away from *this-* the proposal that never should have happened, the pressure from his mom, my issues, and all of his.

He thought he could start a new life in Europe, studying abroad and reaching toward new opportunities. That was the front he put up. But it was a pattern he had.

It was running away all the same.

"I'm serious," he said, trying to move past my accusation. "I can do school, and maybe you can too. Find something you love and study it for a while."

I took my hand away.

"That's what I've been trying to tell you, though. I don't *want* to throw myself back into studying. The same thing is going to happen," I tried to explain, even though I knew not a word was getting through to him.

"No, it wouldn't. We'd make sure it didn't," Andy assured.

We kept getting back into this conversation. This is what we had fought about for months now. I would yell and try to make him hear me, but he never did.

He didn't understand because he wasn't the one who had been slowly ripping themselves apart for months. That was me. I was the one who was struggling to see the point in life.

"This," I said, pointing between both of us, "is why I

know we won't work. I'm trying to focus on life again, on simply being alive. But you're so focused on *doing* something, *achieving* something, which is great! You're doing great, and I'm so proud of you. But I know you won't settle for me just living. You need me out there thriving."

"No," he insisted, a shadow crossing his face. He stood up so he could be in front of me. "Beck, you know I'm here for *you*. Not your accomplishments."

I almost believed him. Because, to an extent, he was right. He would never admit aloud that he was ashamed of how little I do. But I saw the way it bothered him. I could see it when he got that funny look on his face like he wanted to tell me to strive for more in my life. I could see it in the way he would tense up when he introduced me to a scholar at the aerospace conferences he'd bring me to. I was always closed out from his world of success, pushed behind a curtain because I was no match for his academics.

He may not have admitted it, but it wasn't in my head.

I forced a slight smile, trying to show him I wasn't mad. I wasn't angry; it was just how things were.

"You've been great to me. Better than I could have asked for. But I saw the way your face dropped when I told you I'm not taking Med next year. I saw the way you stammered when you tried to defend me to your mom. It's like you're trying to convince yourself."

He shook his head.

"I mean, that's what this whole wedding is about anyway,

right?" I continued. "To prove to your mom that you love me? To prove that you can do enough for the both of us?"

"That's because I *have* to do enough for both of us!" he exclaimed. "You're capable of so much. I know you are. But you push things off. You set deadlines that you'll just push back. You keep pushing and pushing until the best years of your life are empty! Don't you see the issue in that?"

"No, I don't. Because I'll die if I make life out to be some big checklist, crossing off goals as I push myself to do them. It's not worth it if I end up hating my life in the process."

Some people postpone for their sanity. Others race because they've already lost theirs.

That's what Andy would never understand.

I stood up so I could hold his face. "What kind of life are we setting up for ourselves? You with a wife that you can't be proud of, and me with a husband who makes me feel like I'm never enough. What kind of life is that?"

I didn't realize I had started crying until he wiped the tears from my chin.

"You've grown so much," I continued. "You've grown into this beautiful person, and I just feel like I'm holding you back."

He shook his head. "You could never hold me back."

"You don't see it yet, but I already am."

"We'll be fine. Don't you want to be with me? Don't you want to get away from this? You can get away from this school, and you can do whatever you need to do. Don't you want that?

Don't you want to fight for this?" he asked.

I fought against his grip.

"Stop that!" I exclaimed, my voice loud and booming. "Stop manipulating me!"

I used to love his sweet talk, all the things he assured me of, all the compliments he gave me. But somewhere along the way, his sweet talk turned manipulative.

I don't know how it got to be like that. All the things we used to love about each other were the same reasons we were falling apart.

His eyes squinted together. "What do you mean I'm being manipulative? This is what you want."

"How do you know what I want? Why are you telling me what I want?"

"Because this is what you want." He said it fiercely.

"Not anymore, it's not," I spat out.

"I don't know how to fix us," he admitted.

Those dark eyes were so terrifying. He was drifting off, and the distance was scaring him.

I felt his hands on me, trying to revive us as if holding each other would meld us back into one. But we broke apart, and neither of us could repair the damage.

"I don't think you can fix this one," I said against his chest.

He kissed my hair.

"Okay, then what do you want to do?" he asked, pulling away from me.

I felt cold without his arms wrapped around me.

"Do you want me to stay here? I don't have to go to Europe."

"Yes, you do," I said.

I was scared to look him in the eye. I was afraid to watch him as I ruined everything.

I froze, taking my time as I traced his face with my eyes, memorizing everything about him even though I already knew it by heart.

The dorm room was completely still, and his space posters surrounded us, all the things he'd dreamed of since he was five years old with glow-in-the-dark stars glued to his ceiling.

Shadows from the dimly lit room danced across his face, across his nose, across his lips.

"Call off the wedding," I said.

And the world gaped at me.

He started laughing.

Andy laughed at the bombshell.

I just watched him as he leaned against his bed, laughing like I'd just told the funniest joke in the world. He smiled at all the wrong times.

"Call off the wedding," he repeated, amused.

He laughed again, but I knew it was hurting him.

And then this expression came over his face, like a hopeful pleading.

"Come on, Rebecca. Marry me and come with me. Do it for me."

He smiled this pure, innocent smile that wasn't tainted with shock or anything. He was smiling because he knew I couldn't say no to his smile.

But this time, I had to.

"No."

His face dropped in surprise. He didn't anticipate that.

"You're not even trying to fight for us," he said.

"I've been fighting all this time!" I exclaimed. "If we have to fight this hard, I don't think it's meant to be."

He shook his head in disbelief. "No. You're giving up on us. You're ending it because you're scared. You're not thinking it out."

"I am, though." I stepped toward him. "Andy, what happens again when I fall? I'm going to pull you down."

"No-"

But he started his sentence a little too soon. Halfway through, he recognized the truth and stopped himself. That pause was as hurtful as a slap.

He looked at me differently, suddenly. Like I wasn't the person he used to love. Like I was this other person hiding in Rebecca's body.

It made me want to peel away my skin, layer after layer until it was just my heart. And then maybe he'd find his Beck again.

"Call off the wedding," he said again. I knew he'd keep repeating it long after I left. "No. We're not doing that."

He was so firm about it.

I knew how to change his mind, but it would crush him. I didn't have any other options, though.

"You said you'd give me a free pass," I said. "One thing you'd do for me if I asked."

I was trying so hard to hold it together when I saw his face drop.

"Come on. You can't use that to back out of our marriage!" he shouted.

"Andy, I'm not kidding about this. It's all I've been thinking about, and I know this is the right thing to do. You can't see it right now, but you will."

I took another step toward him as he sat on the edge of the bed. He wrapped his arms around my waist, resting his head on my chest.

That was the last time I'd hold him. The last time our hearts would beat together.

"You said yes," he told me suddenly. I felt the words against my skin. "You said yes when I asked."

"I shouldn't have," I whispered.

"When you were in that green dress, you said you'd spend the rest of your life with me."

Even then, I knew it was a lie.

"I-"

"Why do we do this to each other?" he asked, still holding me. "Pull each other up just to break down in the end?"

And with that, he took the ring off my finger, led me to the door, and slammed it.

the call that ended it all
May 14

He called me at night when I was packing up my room. Without Andy, nothing was keeping me across the country from my family. It was time I went back home and tried to figure things out. I didn't know if my leave of absence would turn into me dropping out indefinitely. I didn't know if I'd regret what happened between Andy and me in a couple of weeks.

But I'd figure it out at home.

I was putting away my CDs when I got the call.

Andy.

I'd already taken away the hearts by his name in my contacts, but I'd left the picture.

It was the picture from the night we went to a restaurant on the way home from the observatory and ordered more cheesecakes than we could stomach. I took a picture of him, laughing as I teased him.

Now, there he was on my phone, smiling with that big smile, his eyes squinted closed in happiness.

I answered, reminding myself to take the picture off his contact after we hung up.

"Hey, Beck," he said. His voice was soft, broken. "I- This probably isn't the best time, but...I just needed to hear from you one more time. Just to make sure you're okay. I don't know."

He wanted to keep rambling. You could hear how much he was dying to. But he just asked if I was okay.

Was I okay?

"This is stupid. I don't know why I asked." He paused. "Actually, I do know. I called because I was listening to the radio, and that song you like came on, and it reminded me of you. And I was going to get wasted with the engineering guys, but I thought about what you said. About me running away from everything, and so I stayed here while they went out. I guess- I guess I just wanted to let you know I'm trying. And it's because of you that I'm doing that."

There was silence for a long time after that.

"I'm glad you called," I said at last. I cleared my throat. "Because I wanted to tell you I'm trying, too. But I was too scared to call you first."

Relief and sadness filled his laugh.

"I drove over to, uh- I drove to that place."

I didn't have to specify for him to know where I was talking about.

It was the place I went when my mind was screaming as I fell apart. It was the place I called him from, sobbing. The place I sat at while we stayed on the phone until he showed up, saving me from the wreck.

"And I was just thinking how far I've come. I'm still not...all the way there." I laughed so he wouldn't hear my tears. "But I'm getting there, and that's because of you."

I sat crossed-legged on my bed, playing with the drawstring on my sweats. My heart was breaking all over again because I knew this was the end.

He called to say goodbye.

Andy wanted our goodbye to be a nice one. Not like how it was the last time we talked, when our bitter words sliced each other into a thousand pieces.

This goodbye was meant to glue us back together.

But really, it would just destroy us all over again.

"So, you're okay?" Andy asked.

"Are you?"

He didn't say anything. Neither did I.

How were we supposed to be okay when we weren't together?

"Well, then," he said. Pain filled his voice. "I guess this is goodbye."

It was almost a question. If there was anything else on my mind, tell it to him now. Keep the conversation going so we wouldn't have to hang up.

"I guess this is goodbye," I repeated. I'd never heard my voice so soft.

There was another long pause of silence. I could hear him breathing on the other end of the line; I think Andy could hear my breaths too.

My heart caught in my throat because I knew he was about to talk again. He was about to end it, once and for all.

"I love you, Roo," he said.

I thought back to the first time he called me that, the day at the beach where we loved each other more than anything in the world. It was weird knowing I'd never hear that stupid nickname again.

"Love you too," I said.

All I'm going to be able to hear for the rest of my life is his smile shattering into a million pieces.

PART 5: CLOSURE

the beginning of the end

"That's a fascinating story," Dr. Sherman says when I've finished.

There it is. I've rehashed all our moments. All of the things that haunt me in the middle of the night. All the things that make me homesick even though I'm back home.

I didn't mean to tell her everything. I meant to stop before the crash, and the breakup, and everything else that ruined us. But once I got talking, there was no way to stop.

"Do you feel better?"

"I feel lighter."

She nods.

But I also feel like crying again.

"Would you change things if you could?" She looks thoughtful, reminiscing of her own heartbreaks.

"I'd change parts. I can see a lot of aspects where, if we'd handled things differently, maybe we'd still be together. I would go back and communicate with him better because we were really something special."

"You were." Dr. Sherman smiles.

"But for the most part, no. I wouldn't change a thing," I say.

"Then I'd say you're getting there just fine. It'll take time. More time than they pretend it takes in the movies. So don't be too hard on yourself."

My eyes are full of tears.

"I don't like who I am without him," I admit.

"Rebecca, you're dealing with trauma, PTSD, and heartbreak at the same time. And that takes a toll on a person. So, take your time, be kind to yourself. Maybe it's not that you don't like yourself without him. You're just adjusting to the person you're becoming."

I nod, her words resonating deep in my chest.

"So, what do I do now?"

"Get the happily ever after you deserve." She smiles in a way that makes me believe that I can do anything I set my mind to.

the west coast

It's weird to see people pass you on the streets and realize they have fully formed, complex lives, just as substantial as yours. They're all daughters and sons of someone; they're brothers and sisters, friends and enemies.

They're going through heartbreak, depression, and hardship.

They're human, just like you, and you're not the only one feeling like you've hit rock bottom, even though you feel like you are.

Sometimes I try to make identities for these strangers that I see. While June and I walk down the beach, I assign characteristics and motivations to the people I pass.

That girl, the one with the sunburn and the baseball cap, she's trying to lose weight that she doesn't have. She runs down the beach all day, every day, trying to shed the pounds in her head. She feels dizzy and light-headed, but she makes herself run another stretch. She won't eat a bite of food until she does.

That guy, the one who still has sand on his legs, is coming back from the beach. He surfs there every day to calm his ferocious mind.

And him, he's the one that plays chess under the tree because that's where he and his wife used to sit before she died.

The list goes on and on, and I give names and faces to everyone.

I wonder what stories people make up about me.

"Do you miss Boston?" June asks.

I've been home for almost two months now.

"Not as much as I thought I would," I answered. "This year, things just weren't right. I've felt it for a while. I wasn't cut out for Pre-Med. That stuff takes a toll on you, and I wasn't ready to see people die. And with everything that happened with Andy...Andy is what made Boston home."

June nods.

I smile to make things lighter. "I liked the cold weather, but there's nothing like the feeling of being back in California. The sun never felt so good."

"You got that right."

We hold our shoes in our hands as we walk down the shore. The water laps at our feet, making our toes stick with wet sand. Seagulls fly overhead.

"I heard Mom talking with her friends. They asked if you're going back in the fall."

"I don't know. But I'll figure it out, June Bug."

"Do you feel like your other half is missing? That's how they always phrase it in the movies."

I shake my head. "No. I was whole before him, and I'll be whole after him. But when I was with Andy, we were two wholes. It's like I upgraded."

"One more question, and then I'll stop," June says.

"Promise?" I say cheerily.

There's that smile.

"Promise. Are you over Andy?"

"No. Sometimes I think I almost am," I say. "But then I'll see the trailer for the movie he was so excited to watch, or I'll pass Hazy's and think about the first time we met. The nights are hard because I know he's out there, looking up at the same stars I'm watching. And then I'm right back in the middle of it all. I love him and lose him a million times a day."

June sighs.

"They claim wounds heal with time, but when you have a wound so deep, when you come off of a love as strong as ours, I don't know how you can ever recover. Not fully. At least, that's what I used to think. But I've been optimistic lately. Therapy is helping, especially with PTSD. And I think I'll get to the point where things will be okay. I have no doubt about that."

I wrap my arm around her neck.

"Now, *please*, let's get back to our fun afternoon. Tell me about the drama with Joshua and Opal. I'm dying to hear updates," I say.

"I'm so glad you asked!" she beams. "Joshua and Opal have gotten into *so* much trouble lately..."

We spend the whole afternoon talking about Joshua and Opal, her hopes for junior year, and the latest gossip in town and in the magazines.

I take her hand in mine, feeling the way she constantly trembles from her breathing medication.

"I miss this," I tell her. "College isn't what it's cracked up to be. *This* is where the real fun is."

There's a sudden shout as a guy almost barrels into us, diving to catch a frisbee. He calls out a warning, and we dodge his body just in time.

He stands up and apologizes. We wave it off and go our separate ways.

I can't help but think maybe he's a college student

himself, just as lost as I am. But at the beach, he doesn't have to worry so much about his future. Maybe he has a girlfriend who loves him. Maybe he doesn't. I bet his name is Sean.

"Have you ever had that feeling when you realize that you're just an extra in some stranger's life? Like, the same way you're looking at them and thinking their only purpose is to pass you as you drink coffee or to run into you while you're walking down the beach...they're thinking the same thing about you?"

"Sonder," June says.

"What's that?"

"The word for that feeling. It means you realize the people you pass have ambitions and dreams and *lives* just like yours."

The sun is setting, and it casts a glow on her skin. She looks so wise, so magical, with that golden shine.

"Sonder," I repeat.

my wedding that isn't mine

"Did you hear about Carlotta?" June exclaims, running into my room.

I nod. "Andy texted me yesterday."

"Hold up. He texted you? And you didn't tell me?" She looks offended.

"We didn't say much. He apologized for his mom and

said she was hijacking our wedding. There wasn't much else to say."

There is a lot I wanted to talk to him about. I was almost excited when I saw his text; there was so much I could tell him. But things were over.

We were civil if you could call it that.

And that was all.

"You're okay with that? I mean, Carlotta has done a lot of crap, but stealing her son's wedding is on a whole other level! Are you going to the wedding?"

"Going to the wedding that was supposed to be mine, where my ex's mother is marrying a hitman? That's a little too much drama for my comfort zone."

"Is Andy going?"

Mom's threatening to cut me off if I don't go.

It was such a simple text after he broke the news. I've read it over a million times, and I don't think he was asking for permission. Knowing Andy, he wanted to feel me out, to see if I'd hate him if he goes. But I wouldn't hate him, not even if he attends our wedding.

You should go.

There was so much I wanted to tell him. But I left it at that.

For the record, you looked better in a wedding dress than she ever could.

That made me smile.

"Yeah, Andy's going," I say.

I feel bad for him. He's going to have to sit there at the wedding I called off.

That's a torture I don't wish on anyone.

lavender smoke

It's the night of what would have been my wedding, and I plan to spend the night alone in my room. I'm already thirty minutes into my playlist.

I look at the candles June gave to me. There's either glitter, or coffee grounds, or flower petals in each one. She's made them extra beautiful for me, and it makes me happy to see how her candle shop is thriving.

I light the Lavender Woods candle and place Champagne Toast beside it in honor of the ruined festivities.

I wear the orchid tie-dye sweatshirt that I bought from the mall last week. It's the same one Andy has, the one I borrowed a million times during the length of our relationship. It's the one I wanted even before I went off to college.

I don't know when that article of clothing started symbolizing me taking life back into my own hands, but I feel so much better wearing it.

As I'm sitting in my room, I think of what the wedding must be like. I wonder if he's there, wishing I was in the reception hall. Spotting my face in the crowd would immediately calm him.

He's never done well with crowds.

I go to the kitchen and fill a plate with the food Mom made for me. It's the comfort food June asked Mom to make, specifically for me, to soothe my stomach while I try to soothe my soul.

It smells so good- the beef and spice of yukgaejang, the pork and soy of mandu. I take it to my room and eat it while I work through my problems.

Rock music blares in my headphones.

Dr. Sherman said I should keep a journal, a place where I can write things down. So, I take her advice and start scribbling in the pages.

I eat while I write. I write down every complaint I have about our relationship, the things I wish we did differently, the good times we had, and how we saved each other.

Teardrops smudge the ink.

I get through eighteen pages before I stop writing.

I sit with the essay of us in my hand, and I watch it burn. All my words light up in flames.

I watch everything go up in smoke.

All the unsaid words, all the things I could never bring myself to admit out loud, are swirling around me, poisoning my lungs and lifting the burden off my chest.

I breathe in the smoke and the lavender scent.

It's the scent of closure.

I go through all the stages of grief at once.

And then, finally, the sadness doesn't come back. Neither

does the anger. It's just me, my dried tears, and the candles.

Andy's not haunting me anymore. He's no longer the only thing on my mind.

Now I'm thinking of myself. I think of what I'll do when fall comes around. I think of who I'll be without him at my side.

I get a text and look at my phone.

It's Hillary.

I'm outside your house. Let's go to a concert.

She must be kidding. The last time I talked to her, she was in Boston.

I call her.

"Rebecca!" she exclaims. "Palm Trees and Powerlines are playing in town tomorrow, so I came early and got us tickets for a new punk band. I couldn't leave my best friend alone on her canceled wedding night. So, come on!"

"I'm literally in my sweats right now, and I've been crying for half the night. I wouldn't call this concert material," I say.

"You're always concert material. Don't even get ready. Just get your shoes on, and we'll head out."

"Are you kidding?"

"Nope. Come out, or I'm gonna have to drag you out," Hillary warns. "Bring Griffin and June, too. I know the club manager; he'll let them in."

I almost say no. But then I think of the goal Dr. Sherman gave me for the week. *Do one thing you don't want to do.* She thinks I'm closing off from people, that my guilt is causing me to punish myself subconsciously. She told me to do one thing that was outside of my comfort zone.

My comfort is telling me to stay home and continue crying.

"Okay, let me go get June and Griffin," I say.

Dr. Sherman will be proud of me when I tell her next session.

And so, the three of us Dae kids go out to the driveway, still in our pajamas, where Hillary waits in her cherry red convertible for us.

"That's what I'm talking about!" she hollers when she sees us.

We drive with the top down, the music blaring. June and Griffin are ecstatic in the backseat.

We pull up to the venue, and just like Hillary promised, the bouncer lets inside, no questions asked. She leads us to the front of the crowd, telling June and Griffin what to expect.

They both look so happy, and I'm grateful Hillary did this for us.

I haven't been to a concert in a long time, and it reminds me of the show I anticipated the most: Red Light's goodbye tour. The one I missed because of the shooting.

Dr. Sherman's right. I've been punishing myself. I've punished myself for not saving the man, for not being the one who died at the gas station.

But it feels like home being at a concert. And even though concerts will always bring back the painful memories of this past winter, I know this is where I should be right now. It's one step toward peace.

"Thank you for this!" I shout over the band.

"Glad I could help," she says.

June and Griffin have never been to a concert before. This is their first, and they love it.

We all dance and forget our problems.

I've never felt so liberated, singing with Hillary, and watching my siblings have the time of their life. I don't care that my eyes are still swollen, that I'm wearing sweats and no makeup, and that I don't have a boy by my side.

In the middle of the haze and flashing lights, I jump and smile, realizing this is what acceptance feels like.

There's been a distance between me and my feelings lately. I don't feel like I'm living. I feel like I'm wandering, trying to find something to make me feel alive again.

Med classes may not be the thing that brings me joy anymore, but maybe I'll find a new path to follow. Maybe I'll find a field of passion elsewhere, something that I'm meant to pursue.

Andy may not be the one who comforts me anymore, but I'm starting to step into that role myself. And maybe down the road, there'll be a new someone who loves me and who I love back.

There's so much I don't know.

But I do know that at this moment, with Hillary and my siblings, I feel alive. I haven't felt this good in a long time.

So, for now, I need to focus on the way my heart beats

with adrenaline, the way my cheeks hurt from smiling, and the way my feet ache from jumping.

I'm on the mend, and I can feel it in my bones.

I'm on the come-up.

And more than anything, I know I'll be okay.

I see happiness in my future.

ACKNOWLEDGEMENTS

Thank you, loyal readers, for supporting a book so near and dear to my heart. Without you, I wouldn't have the opportunity to share these characters with the world. You all are incredible for giving me an outlet, and I will always be grateful for that privilege.

An extra special thanks to Mom and Papa for putting up with my endless writing during the days- and nights. Mom, thank you for keeping me grounded throughout my writing process and believing that I can do anything I put my mind to.

Thank you to my friends, especially Raegan, for letting me bounce my ideas off you, and for offering feedback so I can improve in my writing journey.

I am so happy to share my second novel with you beautiful people. Thank you for welcoming these characters into your lives.